What the press says about Harlequin Romances…

"…clean, wholesome fiction…always with an upbeat, happy ending."
—*San Francisco Chronicle*

"…a work of art."
— *The Globe & Mail,* Toronto

"Nothing quite like it has happened since *Gone With the Wind…*"
—*Los Angeles Times*

"…among the top ten…"
—*International Herald-Tribune,* Paris

"Women have come to trust these clean, easy-to-read love stories about contemporary people, set in exciting foreign places."
—*Best Sellers,* New York

OTHER
Harlequin Romances
by JANE DONNELLY

The
Black Hunter

by

JANE DONNELLY

Harlequin Books

TORONTO • LONDON • NEW YORK • AMSTERDAM • SYDNEY

Original hardcover edition published in 1978
by Mills & Boon Limited

ISBN 0-373-02187-9

Harlequin edition published August 1978

CHAPTER ONE

'I HOPE you know what you're doing,' Simon Holcroft said very quietly to his sister, and she laughed,

'I should do, shouldn't I? At my age.'

She was twenty-six and could have passed for twenty anywhere, a long-legged girl, with a clear skin and grey-blue eyes and a mane of silky sun-streaked brown hair. In features she looked very like her brother, although at thirty there were lines on his face.

Dora's forehead was smooth and her wide mouth curved, smiling while she asked, 'Don't you think it's time I settled down?'

'I suppose so.'

'Don't you like Neil?' As Neil Hewitt was just the other side of the door she had to whisper that and Simon said,

'Yes, I like him.'

There wasn't much to dislike about Neil, who was nice-looking, intelligent and wholly reliable. Dora had been his secretary for the last two years—he was an accountant—and dating him for ages.

She suspected he would have proposed to her before now if his mother hadn't had doubts about Dora Holcroft as a daughter-in-law. Of course no girl would have quite satisfied Mrs Hewitt, and in the old days, before the money ran out, she would have been happier to welcome Dora.

There was no money now, Dora was a working girl with only her salary, and Mrs Hewitt considered her flighty because she had been engaged twice before. Almost married once, with the wedding date fixed, and then she had developed cold feet and called the whole thing off.

This was a small Wiltshire village and that sort of thing was remembered. But now Dora was wearing Neil's ring—his mother's, actually, to denote her seal of approval—and this time there would be no last-minute panic.

That had been the trouble before. She had reached a stage where she had known that she couldn't marry the man. She had thought she loved each of them in their turn, and then the slow build-up of doubts had begun, and she had tried to understand what was worrying her.

She was warm and gay and generous, she couldn't be afraid of love. It had to be marriage she was afraid of, promising until death, because at the end all she could do was hand back the engagement ring and say, 'I'm sorry, I can't go through with it. I don't know why, but I do know it wouldn't work. Please forgive me.'

They hadn't forgiven her for a long time; nobody enjoys being jilted. But by now one of the men was married and the other had moved away, and for eighteen months Dora had been seeing Neil, out of the office as well as in it, and for the last six months he had been her sole and steady date.

When he first took her home she got a chilly reception. His mother was a widow and Neil was the apple of her eye, everything in that neat and shining bungalow was geared to Neil. There were photographs of him everywhere, the books were his books, his hi-fi half filled the living room. Mrs Hewitt spent the whole of that first evening discussing the illnesses that had dogged his childhood—he seemed to have been an unlucky as well as a delicate child, he hadn't missed much. He looked healthy enough now, but his mother still pressed herbal tablets on him when he cleared his throat once.

Dora wondered if she was being warned that Neil could be a full-time nursing job, but he smiled good-humouredly at his mother, and apologised later that she fussed over him. He probably wouldn't expect his wife to do the same. 'You know what mothers are,' he said.

'Oh yes,' said Dora, although her mother had died when she was a baby.

After a few visits Mrs Hewitt brought out the photograph albums and Neil explained that that was a sign that she was beginning to take to Dora. Lately she had been quite affable, and she had accepted an invitation to tea in Dora's home, her sharp eyes inspecting the furniture and the polish on it.

Dora had done a thorough clean and shine up before she'd asked Mrs Hewitt round. The little house looked charming and Dora produced some excellent home baking, and Mrs Hewitt seemed reassured.

Neil had proposed to Dora just a week ago. They had been out for a meal and Neil stopped the car on the way home, pulling in at the top of a hill, by daylight a venue for tourists who came to see the beaked white horse from pre-history, carved in the hillside. At night it was romantic up here, as the horse glimmered in the moonlight and the twinkling lights of villages spread out below.

Dora liked being kissed goodnight. She liked the feel of Neil's arms around her, and his comforting un-demanding kisses. Neil never went too far, and Dora appreciated that; she felt they were building up a good relationship. Everything in its time.

Tonight he said, as he looked at her in the crook of his arm with her long brown hair flowing out around her, 'I love you.'

'I love you,' she said drowsily. Neil's kisses often made her feel drowsy. But this time that didn't seem to satisfy him, he was breathing faster and the arms around her suddenly held her tighter, and she thought —oh dear, I don't think I'm ready for this, when he said,

'Let's get married.'

She had been expecting it. She had already decided that life with Neil would go on much the same as now, and she could see nothing wrong with that. She enjoyed her life and she loved Neil. He had a few faults, but who hasn't? She certainly had hers. If he was prepared to bear with her she would be very happy to be married to him.

She said, 'All right,' and he kissed her again, a kiss that hardly differed at all from the kisses that had gone before. Then he turned on the ignition key and said, 'Let's tell Mother.'

Mother knew. She was waiting, with three glasses and a bottle of sparkling wine on the table, and as they went into the hall she came to meet them, folding Dora in a brief embrace and kissing her cheek. 'Dora's going to marry me,' said Neil.

His mother kissed him then, and looked at him proudly as though any girl would be lucky to get him. She actually said, 'Dora's a very lucky girl,' before she said, 'and you're a lucky boy, and I just pray you're both going to be happy.'

They drank to their future happiness and Mr

Hewitt produced a ring in a ring box, and Neil said, 'Mother, are you sure?' This did seem to surprise him, although it was obvious they had discussed the proposal well ahead.

'I want Dora to have it,' Mrs Hewitt said. 'It's an old family ring, Dora, and I always thought I'd like to hand it on to Neil's wife.'

'It's beautiful,' said Dora, and it was, a row of rubies in an antique setting.

Neil said, 'If it doesn't fit you I can get it altered. May I?' He put it on and it fitted very well, and Mrs Hewitt said graciously,

'It could have been made for you. I do like the old designs. I've got several pretty things that will be coming to you one day.'

Into Dora's mind came the memory of other 'pretty things' that had belonged to her mother. Her father had sold them, all but the string of pearls he had given her on her sixteenth birthday, and she hadn't had those for long.

She had shivered suddenly and Mrs Hewitt, who had been holding her hand admiring the ring, had said, 'You're not cold, are you? Not catching a chill? It is draughty in that house of yours, but this is a nice warm house, we'll all be comfortable in here.'

She was taking it for granted they would live together, and Dora knew there would be trouble if they did; but with an heirloom ring on her finger and both Neil and his mother smiling at her she couldn't spoil the euphoric moment. Later she would have to suggest to Neil that he and she lived in her house, or found themselves a flat.

She went down to the shop next day to show Simon and his wife her ring, and tell them the news. They

had a small antique shop, with a flat over it, and Thea
said this was no surprise to her. Dora was very fond of
Thea, and they hugged each other and went into a
huddle over the ring.

'That's pretty,' said Thea, with the eye of an expert
on antique jewellery.

'Where did he get it from?' Simon demanded. 'We
could have sold him a very nice ring.'

'Mrs Hewitt gave it to me,' Dora explained, and
Simon gave a hoot of laughter and Thea said warn-
ingly,

'Simon!'

'Well, he is a bit of a mum's boy, isn't he?' Simon
grinned at his wife and his sister. He had the Holcroft
charm. He and Dora made a striking pair, with the
same silky hair and wide-spaced eyes. He had had
promise of a great career, he was going to be a bar-
rister, but instead he had ended up in the little antique shop, married to Thea and with a baby at last
after nearly nine years.

Dora thought he had done well. If anyone had suggested otherwise she would have been fiercely defen-
sive because Thea, practical and pretty, had made him
a marvellous wife, and the shop gave them a comfortable living, and Clare was the prettiest baby ever.

She was proud of Simon, she always had been. He
had done all right. All their plans had had to change
when their father died and they found what a fool's
paradise they had been living in, but Simon and Thea
were making a good life for themselves.

Simon had cast a critical eye over all Dora's young
men, and there was no reason why Neil should escape.
Simon always teased her. He had teased her over her
ring, and he was teasing her now, asking her if she

knew what she was doing. Joking, because Neil had just gone into the kitchen to help Thea with the washing up.

Dora had cooked the meal they had just eaten, because it was her afternoon off from work, and they had had a little dinner party, the four of them, in Simon and Thea's flat. It had been a good meal, steak and the trimmings followed by cheesecake and a bottle of wine. Neil had been here before, but this was the first time since the engagement was announced, and it was a celebration.

When Thea began to clear away Dora got up too, and Thea said, 'No, you've done your share.'

Neil had agreed. 'You certainly have—it was delicious.' He'd offered, 'I'll give you a hand with the dishes,' and went off with a pile of plates into the kitchen.

Thea said, 'Thank you,' and Simon said,

'Good lad,' and got a face pulled at him by Thea. She thought Neil Hewitt was eligible and anxious to please, and she hoped that Dora would be a match for Mrs Hewitt. She had a feeling that Neil was going to ask for an apron in the kitchen, and that would have convulsed Simon, so she closed the door when she carried in the tray.

'One of the nice things about Neil,' said Dora now, 'is that he's considerate.'

'Yes.' Simon could hardly have denied it, but he suddenly looked almost serious. 'It's just that I'm not sure you're the marrying type.'

She hadn't been up to now, but this time she would go through with it and she would make Neil a good wife. Simon had said that before, and always she had hoped he wasn't talking about himself. They had so much in common: looks, likes and dislikes. Often she felt she knew what Simon was thinking, and he had always been her best friend as well as her brother.

But she had never been jealous of Thea. She might have been. She had only lost her father a few months when she lost her brother to Thea, except that it hadn't been like that.

It was after their father died that Simon brought Thea home for the first time. He had met her in Oxford, where he was studying for his law degree and she was working in an antique shop. She was wearing a Laura Ashley dress, a big kind girl, with a velvety complexion and goodness brimming over, and Dora had loved her on sight. When Simon had said they were getting married it had seemed to Dora the best thing that could possibly happen. Thea was loving and sensible and good, and Dora's early impressions of her sister-in-law had been borne out a hundred times.

Simon couldn't have done better no matter how long he had searched for a wife, but he had married young and when he said, 'You're not the marrying type,' Dora wondered if sometimes he was imagining himself without ties.

The shop was delightful, but running it and attending auctions was hardly a madly exciting life, and now there was the responsibility of the baby, and nobody is entirely satisfied with their lot. Dora said quietly, 'If I'm half as lucky as you in my marriage I'll thank heaven on my knees,' and Simon said,

'You're right there,' and there was no doubt at all that he meant it. He just needed it pointing out to him occasionally.

Thea came back with a tray of coffee cups and

dumped it in front of Simon, smiling, 'Put these around, if you've got the strength!'

'I had a hard day,' he said.

He had been to a sale, returning after closing time with several pieces they hoped were bargains, and Thea laughed.

'Did I tell you about the coach party?' She had. They didn't often get coach parties, but this afternoon this coach had had a fortuitous puncture just down the road and an astonished Thea had found her shop packed to the door.

It wasn't likely to happen again in years. She had called up to Dora, who was in the kitchen crumbling wholemeal biscuits for the cheesecake base at the time, and together the two girls had done a brisk business in small lines.

The four of them sat down again now, drinking their coffee and chatting, when the phone rang in the little hall of the flat. Simon took it and called, 'Neil!'

'For me?' Neil went along to take the call and Simon came back and sat down again, grinning.

'It's your mother-in-law.'

'I hope everything's all right,' said Dora.

'Probably checking what time wandering boy will be home,' said Simon.

'Oh, that reminds me.' Thea clapped a hand to her forehead. 'It went straight out of my mind, but there was a phone call this afternoon—about the house. It seems it's probably sold.'

They didn't have to ask which house. The Manor, of course, and Simon and Dora exchanged glances with the same expression of wry resignation, the same small shrug and half sigh.

They had sold the Manor and the meadow ten years

ago. What was left had gone to buy a lease on this shop and to keep Dora through her commercial training until she began to earn a living. There hadn't been much because there had been big debts.

It had been run as a guesthouse, but recently the owner had died and his wife had put it on the market, and Dora and Simon had played a game of let's pretend we can buy it back.

Of course they knew they couldn't. If there was an auction of contents then they would turn up and perhaps put in a few bids. There might be something they could sell in the shop. But in hard cash they hadn't enough to buy a cottage, let alone a small manor house, and even if they had had there could have been no going back.

That style of living was over for them. They would never again be the Holcrofts of the Manor, but it had been fun to go and look over the place. The estate agent was a friend of theirs, and he had suggested they might like to see it.

Neither had been inside since they sold it, and the years had rolled on until the present became more important than the past, and when John Redway said did they want to see over the old place again they had been curious, no more.

It was hardly recognisable, but they walked around saying, 'Do you remember ...?' and, 'This was the old nursery,' and, 'The view's still the same from this window,' and came out, with Thea and John, in a mellow mood of nostalgia.

'Let me know if you want to buy it,' John had said, smiling because he knew they didn't and they couldn't, and they had all gone into Dora's house for supper and started playing the pretend game.

'If we ever did go back,' Simon had said, 'we could run the business from there, use the rooms for settings for antiques. It might bring the tourists in.'

'It went all right as an hotel,' Dora had said. 'Well, not too badly.' The owner's ill health had made things difficult this last year. 'We might run it as a family. I could do the cooking and Thea could organise everything, and you could dig the garden and wear a velvet jacket in the evenings and play mine host.'

'The first thing we buy, when we win the pools,' said Thea.

None of them did the pools, but Simon said, 'Right. As soon as we get the money we'll buy the Manor.'

It was never anything but a joke, but Dora suspected that Thea had held back the news that it was sold until they had eaten their meal, and drunk a glass or two of wine, and the strains of the day had ebbed.

They knew they couldn't have their own home back again, but the fact that someone else was moving in gave them both a little pang of regret. While the house stood still they could people it with memories. They could have gone along again any time and walked through it again.

'What's happening to it?' Dora asked.

It was unlikely to become a private dwelling house again. Somebody probably had plans to run it on a business basis. Thea said, 'John didn't say. Just that somebody was interested and he thought he might have a sale, and the man said he knew you and he asked after you. His name was Sullivan.'

Brother and sister looked blankly at each other, then Dora's eyes widened and Simon whistled almost soundlessly. 'It couldn't be,' he said.

Dora shook her head. Her 'No' was very emphatic.

'Who?' Thea leaned forward, intrigued.

'Coll Sullivan,' said Simon, slowly as though he hadn't said the name for a long time and he wasn't sure how it sounded.

'Who's he?' demanded Thea.

Neither answered for a moment, then Simon said, 'He was a gipsy. He used to camp off the main road.' There was a pull-in just outside the village where the trailer-caravans still came two or three times a year, staying a week or two until they were moved on.

'Not a gipsy,' said Dora. 'A tinker.'

'... Not gipsy-scum, tinker-scum,' he had said, 'and this time I won't be back ...'

'*No!*' she said again, and Simon asked,

'Do you know another Sullivan?'

'I don't think so, but I could do.'

Thea smiled. 'Well, if he's thinking of buying the Manor he's come a long way. What was his line?'

'His father dealt in scrap metal, old bangers, that sort of thing.' Simon shrugged. 'Junk.'

'Perhaps he's made a fortune out of scrap.' Thea was finding this very interesting. 'What was he like?'

Simon was doing the answering. Dora sat, turning the ring on her finger. 'My age,' said Simon. 'He came with his father.' He did some mental calculations. 'Oh, about half a dozen times in about ten years.'

Four times. Dora could have told them. She remembered exactly.

'He'd be about twenty when we saw him last.' Simon was remembering again, too, how Coll Sullivan had looked and sounded when he last came to this village. 'You know,' said Simon, his voice rising, 'I wouldn't be all that surprised if it is him.'

A thin wail came out of the little baby-alarm that

connected with the mike hanging over the cot. It didn't sound urgent, as though Clare was stirring in her sleep rather than waking, but Dora jumped up. 'Can I?'

'Sure,' said Thea. 'But I think she'll go off again.'

Clare—usually referred to and addressed as Kiki—was a happy baby. Sleeping and waking she was more delight than trouble. As Dora opened the door into the hall she almost bumped into Neil, who told them, 'Mother wasn't sure whether I said I'd be bringing you home for supper.'

'Not before midnight,' said Simon.

'Just looking in on Kiki.' Dora gave Neil a quick smile. 'I'll be back in a minute.'

She went into the nursery, closing the door quietly, and going over to the cot where Kiki was lying peacefully, sprawled in relaxed baby slumber. Flushed with sleep, damp golden curls sticking to her forehead, she was a picture.

Dora wished she had woken. She would have liked to pick her up and cuddle her close, and not just because she loved her, but because it would have been comfort for her, as well as the child, to have something warm and loving in her arms.

She was feeling strange, shaken. It was like that old saying about something walking over your grave. Little icy shivers were running down her spine, and she went across to the window, pulling a curtain back, looking up and down the road.

She couldn't stay in here for long. She would have to go back and say that Kiki was sleeping, and they would still be talking about the chance of the Manor being sold, and the man who might buy it.

If he bought it, of course. There was many a slip

between an interested viewer and a signed contract, and if it should be Coll Sullivan it was always possible that he'd seen an advertisement and asked to look over the place from sheer curiosity. It didn't mean he had that kind of money or wanted that kind of house.

She wondered what the years had done to him. Ten years were enough to change him out of recognition. He would be older, of course, settled maybe. He could have children almost as old as he had been when he first came to this village.

She couldn't imagine him now. She could see him vividly as he was the four times he came here, between the ages of ten and twenty. Each time there was a separate and detailed picture, but she couldn't imagine beyond the young man with the black hair and the hawk face who had looked at her with such contempt.

No one else had ever looked at her like that. Not even the man whose ring she had returned after the wedding invitations had been sent out.

'This time I won't be back,' Coll had said. But this afternoon he could have been walking through the grounds and the rooms of the Manor. If it was Coll.

She tried to think. Sullivan ... *Sullivan* ... Surely she knew another Sullivan? It might be someone she or Simon had met through business, a client of Neil's or somebody who had bought something from the shop sometime. Someone the estate agent didn't know. But, try as she would, no one came to mind.

The street was almost empty, and she would have to go back into the living room or Thea would be along to see what was holding her up. By now they might have finished discussing the sale.

But she still stood there, watching each car, each

pedestrian, her eyes darting as though she was on look-out. And then a car drew up just outside, and she knew that she was at this window because she had wanted to be prepared, she had had an instinctive feeling he would be seeking them out.

Of course this could be another visitor, a friend, although she couldn't recognise the car. And expensive cars did draw up beside antique shops, even closed ones, so that passengers could look into windows.

One man got out. He stood back and looked up, and he was Coll Sullivan and Dora thought she was going to choke.

She shrank back from the window, and stood for a frozen moment. Her blood was ice and her teeth were chattering. Then she hurried from the room, and along the little passage to where they were still sitting around the table.

'Hey,' she said brightly, 'did you hear the car?'

'What car?' asked Simon.

'The one that's just drawn up outside.' The bell rang and she said, 'Get ready for a surprise—it *is* Coll Sullivan.'

'Well, what d'y'know?' said Simon.

'Who?' asked Neil.

'The man who might be buying the Manor,' said Dora. 'Haven't they told you?'

'It isn't actually sold yet, is it?' said Thea. 'And Neil's been telling us his mother wants us all to go over to the bungalow sometime. We've been trying to work out when.'

What she really meant was that Simon had been raising objections to every date put forward. Simon had gone downstairs to answer the door, and Thea said, 'This *is* exciting. I'm looking forward to meeting him.'

'What's exciting?' Neil demanded.

'He used to come to the village years ago,' Thea explained. 'Didn't he?' Dora nodded.

'What's he going to do with the Manor?' Neil wanted to know, and Dora shrugged.

'John Redway, the estate agent, phoned through this afternoon,' said Thea, 'to say he thought he might have a sale. That's all we know.'

Simon was doing the talking, it was his voice and his laughter that reached them, welcome in both. When he pushed open the door he ushered in the visitor with a flourish, and stood back with the pleased expression of an impresario delivering a star. 'Look who we've got here,' he said.

The man stood smiling at them. He was tall, broad-shouldered in a thin grey polo-necked sweater and grey slacks. His eyebrows were raised in amused query, as he looked at the three who were facing him.

Dora would have known him. She would have known him anywhere. 'Hello,' he said. He was speaking to her and she smiled politely.

'This is a surprise.'

So it was. Before she had any inkling what he had in mind he had covered the three paces between them, taken her in his arms and kissed her firmly on the mouth.

She was shocked speechless, and before she could protest or shove he had stepped back and was saying cheerfully, 'It's good to see you again. You haven't changed at all.'

Perhaps she hadn't inside. She had forgotten that confusion of feelings—resentment, anger, perhaps a little fear—that Coll Sullivan had always stirred in her. She still felt the same inside, looking at him, her lips stiff in rejection of the touch of his lips.

But of course her appearance had changed, for the better, she hoped, and she said—pretending to laugh—'Considering I was a scrubbed-face sixteen-year-old when we last met is that supposed to be a compliment?'

He was the only one who didn't laugh. 'No,' he said, 'an observation.' He turned to the others and Simon put an arm around Thea.

'Meet Coll Sullivan,' said Simon. 'One-time gipsy, God knows what now. And this is my wife Thea.'

Coll took Thea's hand and Dora had to admit that he was handsome. The black hair sprang back from a peak and the dark eyes had a spiky fringe of lashes. The nose was high-bridged and the mouth was firm and long. Thea was smiling as though she enjoyed looking at him, saying, 'Hello.'

'And Neil Hewitt, Dora's fiancé,' said Simon.

Coll seemed to let Thea's hand go reluctantly. He turned to Neil and smiled, making a helpless gesture. 'In that case I should be apologising for kissing Dora.' To me you should, Dora thought, because nothing had ever happened to give him the right to kiss her on sight. Even if a lot of years had passed and he looked as though he now took what he wanted.

'But we three were childhood playmates,' said Coll, and his smile was for Simon and Dora, as though all their memories were good.

'*Are* you thinking of buying the Manor?' Simon asked.

'I am buying it.'

Dora's heart sank. In her turmoil of emotion she felt

an extra bit of leaden depression where her heart probably was, but Simon's grin was delighted, if astonished.

'How——' he began, laughing, and Coll prompted,
'How did I get hold of the money?'

'Well, yes,' said Simon.

'Would you believe in luck?'

There was a glittering, reckless look about him. She
remembered that too, and the way he threw back his
head, as though he would enjoy taking on anything or
anyone. It was a dangerous look, although some folk
might describe it as charisma.

I'd believe it, she thought. I'd believe anything of
you. I'd believe murder.

'Well, yes,' said Simon, 'it would have to be luck, of
course but how——?'

'*Simon!*' protested Thea. She turned to Coll, playing the hostess in gay exaggerated fashion. 'Do *please*
sit down, and please can I offer you a drink or something before my husband,' she pretended to glare at
Simon, 'really starts to cross-question you.'

'I'm an open book,' said Coll. He took a chair and
Simon sat down beside him. Then Neil sat down and,
slowly, so did Dora. Coll smiled at Thea. 'I'm driving,
but a coffee would be very acceptable.'

There were no rough edges to his voice now. It was
the same voice, but as free of accent as Simon's. He
looked aristocratic, born to the good life, even his
shoes looked handmade.

He could have been a childhood playmate who had
been brought to the Manor in a chauffeured car, instead of dropping out of the trees like something dark
and wild.

He had landed on his feet like a cat, jumping from
an old walnut tree, as Simon and Dora rode around

the five-acre meadow; and Dora's horse had shied slightly. Dora was six years old, and Folly was a birthday present, a small New Forest pony of whom she was immensely proud.

Right then, all those years ago, she had taken an instant dislike to the dark boy who was Simon's age. At first it might have been because Simon didn't dislike him, and she was jealous.

He camped in the neighbourhood for the best part of a month that first summer, and he turned up again and again, going off with Simon—who was home from boarding school—leaving her behind. But it was the day they all insisted Folly had bolted that she hated him. She still believed she had been in control. There were horses in the stables in those days, Coll was allowed to ride when he had proved to her father, and to Tommy the groom, that he could handle a horse.

The three of them were riding high over the hills when a fluttering scrap of paper spooked Folly, who galloped off. Both Simon and Coll had raced after her, and Coll had reached her first, grabbing the reins, soothing and holding the frightened little pony until she came to a standstill.

Dora had been furious, convinced she could have drawn up before she reached the end of the plain, where the ground began to slope down to the valley. She had snatched back her reins, wriggled back in her saddle well out of Coll's touch, and spat at him, 'I could have stopped, I didn't want you—let go of my horse!'

'All right, kid, keep your hair on,' he'd said, and Simon, who was with them by then, had thanked him and called her a stupid kid, and that summer's day, a long time ago, had been spoiled...

The man who had spoiled it was saying now, 'I'm in property, building, construction.'

'All of them?' Simon asked, impressed for all his raillery.

'They're allied trades.' Coll grinned back. 'You remember the last time I was here?'

'Yes,' said Simon.

Very well, thought Dora, oh *very* well. I had forgotten until now how well.

She looked at him, but he didn't meet her eyes, only Simon's. 'I started soon after that,' he explained. 'With a few hundred I'd managed to save I bought a derelict barn and did it up. That was my first profit and I went on from there.

'I've been lucky all along. I was into construction when the recession came, so I weathered it.' He smiled at them, all except Dora. 'And now I'm very comfortably situated, thank you.'

'Are you a millionaire yet?' she heard herself ask tartly, and he said, in the easy understated way he had described his career to date,

'Not yet. But I will be.'

The extraordinary thing was that she believed him. It was going to happen. You looked at him and you believed it.

Simon said, 'This beats all.' He took a long awed breath, then he added, 'It does, but it shouldn't, because you always were a winner.' A grin spread slowly from ear to ear. 'Hey, do you remember the sports at the fur-and-feather fête? How old were we?'

'You were twelve, you two, I was eight,' said Dora, and Simon nodded.

'Yeah, about that.' He was telling Thea, so that she could share the joke. 'Well, he won the lot, everything—the racing, the long jump, the high jump, the lot. He was there in the line for everything, and every time he came in first.'

Dora had wanted Simon to win, or any of half a dozen friends, and this boy from outside, who shouldn't have been there at all, had won everything, every time. And he had to be cheating, because nobody wins at everything.

She was slipping back into those childhood incidents, remembering her emotions so vividly that it was almost impossible to laugh with Simon and Thea. 'Then, another time, there was the birthday party,' Simon chortled. 'Dora's birthday.'

... Her ninth, they had been thirteen. The picture of that came into detailed focus, down to the white dress she had worn, with small embroidered pink daisies, and the buffet in the marquee on the big lawn.

Coll had arrived a couple of days before, still remembered from his athletic triumphs the previous year, and been invited by Simon to her party. When she had protested her father had overruled her and Coll had been among the guests, conspicuous in tattered shirt and trousers that were too large for him.

'There was a fight,' said Simon, chuckling as he recalled it. 'Coll in the middle, laying about like a trooper. It was a shambles, I'd never enjoyed a birthday party so much in my life.'

Coll clapped both hands to his head, and laughing too Thea said, 'I can imagine. What was it all about?'

'As I recall,' said Coll gravely, 'something to do with the cut of my suit.'

Dora remembered that the party was spoiled. That Coll Sullivan had always spoiled things. When he and his father drove off, in their battered old car towing their battered trailer, that time, she had prayed they would never come back. The man never did. He died before the boy was fourteen, and Coll was twenty before they saw him again.

Simon said, 'You know, I really used to look forward to seeing you. We never knew when you'd be coming, or if you'd be coming, but when you did you certainly livened things up.' Dora hoped he wasn't going into any more happy memories. They bored her. She had never liked Coll Sullivan and she never would. But Simon seemed to have had his fill of the past, and he asked, 'What are you going to do with the Manor?'

'Live in it,' said Coll. 'Do you mind?'

He sounded concerned, and Simon said, 'Mind? No. We'd be glad to see it being used as a home again.'

He was speaking for himself and Dora, but Dora murmured objections. 'It's very large—heating and that. And getting staff.'

'I'll manage,' said Coll, and with money of course he would. He said, 'I'm looking forward to being here, I enjoyed those old days very much.' He was still speaking to Simon, although he did glance briefly at Dora when he said, 'I hope you'll come to the Manor. I'd be glad if you'd look on it as another home. I hope we shall be friends again.'

'We certainly will,' said Simon heartily. He jumped up and clapped Coll on the shoulder, and Thea chimed in with matching enthusiasm,

'But of course, that would be lovely. Things couldn't have worked out better, could they? Are you married, by the way?'

'I'm afraid I never found the time.'

Simon stood back, looking at them all—except Neil,

he was no part of this group-in Simon's eyes. 'Well, this is grand,' said Simon. 'This is really grand.'

Yes, thought Dora, if we want things livened up, stirred up, spoiled. All she knew was that her peace of mind was shattered, because she could never trust Coll Sullivan. He was wealthy now, with all the easy charm of affluence. But she knew what Simon and Thea didn't. Coll Sullivan might not need to steal any more, but under the skin he would always be the taunting thief who had taken her mother's pearls and defied her to prove it.

CHAPTER TWO

MOST of the rest of the evening went on reminiscences, with Simon recalling the old days as though Coll's coming had been a regular highlight of the long summer vacation. Although he had only come three times while they were boys, the last time they were young men.

'I often wondered where you went in the winter time,' said Simon. 'You always came in the summer, I remember, the sun always seemed to be shining.'

Dora remembered dark clouds and winds blowing her hair into her eyes. Strange, she thought, how different our images of those days are, and she wondered how Coll remembered them.

He laughed. 'We kept moving. We had to, we were always being moved on,' and Thea, always kind, always sympathetic, said,

'Well, no one will move you from the Manor, you'll

have a real home there,' as though it was only yesterday that Coll Sullivan had been ordered to pack up
and go.

Dora said crisply, 'But I'm sure you've had a home
for years. You'd hardly be living in the trailer still,
would you?'

His dark eyes seemed black, one corner of his mouth
lifted in a lopsided smile. 'The trailer was a write-off
when my father was killed,' he said quietly.

He had told them the last time he came that he was
no longer with his father, but no one had pressed him
for details. Dora remembered what she had said and
her cheeks flamed now. She muttered, 'I'm sorry.'

'So was I.' After a moment he said, 'I have an apart-
ment in a hotel.'

'And now you want a house?' She spoke slowly,
because it was a puzzle why a bachelor should choose
somewhere as rambling as the Manor. 'I should have
thought you'd have built to your own specifications,'
she said.

'I want this house. For special reasons.' Perhaps
Simon had been recounting them. The times he had
spent here when they were children might have been
an oasis to a tinker child.

'And we couldn't wish for a better neighbour,' said
Simon, while Thea nodded smiling agreement and
asked,

'You're not going back tonight, are you? We've got a
spare room.'

'So has Dora,' Simon grinned, and Neil spluttered,
and Coll's dark eyebrows rose.

'Is that an offer, Dora-Lily?' No one else ever called
her that and she had always hated it. Her name was
Dora Lilias and Simon had told Coll, and Coll had

called her Dora-Lily, and when she flew into a tantrum, screaming, 'That isn't my name!' he had said, 'It is. It's what I'm going to call you.' 'Well, I shan't answer.' 'Please yourself,' he'd said.

She could have screamed at him now, 'Don't call me that!' but she didn't fly into tantrums any more. At her age she hoped that she had her temper under control. She said coolly, 'What do you think?' and he sighed,

'I was afraid not.' And while they were all laughing but Neil, he stood up. 'Anyhow, I do have to get back tonight. It's only just over an hour on the motorway. I'll be back.'

He looked straight at Dora when he said, 'I'll be back,' and she remembered how he had done that, every time but the last. It had always sounded like a threat to her, and it did again.

They all went downstairs together, and Coll got into his gleaming Mercedes and Simon said, 'Smashing car.'

'Smashing shop,' said Coll, 'and extremely smashing wife.'

They blushed becomingly and Simon declaimed 'Good luck comes in different packages.'

'Now that's very true,' said Thea. 'Where did you get that?'

'It just came to me,' said Simon. 'I'm thinking of having it done in pokerwork.'

They were laughing as Coll drove away, Neil without much enthusiasm, and Dora only with her lips, but they sounded a merry group, and Thea said, 'I like him. Why hasn't anyone ever told me about him?'

Dora said, 'I suppose we'd better be off too. It's work in the morning.' She would have preferred to walk home, through the quiet street that wended between houses and fields. She lived the other end of the village. The shop fronted the green, with church and pub, the butchers, the post office, the general store, and a dozen or so houses; and Dora lived in what had once been the lodge of the Manor.

She lived there alone, except for one small dog, and in about two minutes Neil would deposit her and leave her alone, unless he came in for a while.

He thanked Thea and Simon for the meal, reminded them of his mother's invitation, and opened the car door for Dora. As the car pulled away from the kerb he said, 'I don't remember him at all.'

'I don't suppose you do,' said Dora. Neil lived about three miles away, but he had never had anything to do with the tinkers in his childhood. Mrs Hewitt would have gone into shock at the suggestion. If Neil hadn't been at that village fête, eighteen years ago, he had probably never set eyes on Coll.

Dora said, 'He was just a boy who came and went,' and Neil shot her a suspicious glance.

'You three seem to have had high old times together.'

'You sound as though we grew up together.' She moved impatiently in her seat. 'I was nine when he broke up my birthday party. I was sixteen when I saw him next, and that was only briefly. Then he went away and we've heard nothing of him since.'

She was silent for a moment or two. 'I don't suppose I've thought about him in ten years,' she said. 'And I don't suppose Simon has. Until tonight we've never talked about him at all.'

'He's a big number now.' Neil sounded envious, and Dora muttered darkly,

'So he says.'

'Oh, he is.' They stopped beside her house, and Neil said, 'Sullivan Properties—I've heard of them.'

'More than I have.' She flung him an irritated look, she could do without a build-up for Coll Sullivan.

'I could get jealous of a man like that,' said Neil mournfully.

'Well, don't,' she snapped. The future promised to be difficult enough without Neil imagining heaven knows what, and then she realised how peevish she was being and said, 'Please don't. Do you want to come in for a cup of coffee?'

He peered at his watch, and seemed surprised at what he saw there. 'Better not, I didn't realise it was so late.'

Mother would be waiting up, but tonight Dora could have done with some support, a promise that all would be well, that Coll Sullivan would spoil nothing.

'So goodnight,' she said, and got out of the car before he could kiss her goodnight. A quick goodnight peck wasn't going to help. She would have needed some real passion tonight to blot Coll Sullivan from her mind, and passion was not Neil's forte. He was a nice man, he really was, but she never came anywhere near forgetting the world in his arms.

She heard the excited yapping of her small dog as she turned her key in the door, and when she stepped into the house he came bounding to greet her.

He was a bright-eyed Jack Russell, quick to give the alarm if anyone was coming to the house. He had learned the difference between traffic up the drive to the Manor, and steps on the short flagstoned path to the front door of the lodge.

She took him around with her as much as she could, but he did bark a lot, he was a yapper, and as they were supposed to be having a celebration dinner to-night, with Neil, it was important that Kiki wasn't woken up, so Tip had been left at home.

He spent most working days at the shop. He had been Simon and Thea's present to Dora on her birth-day three years ago, arriving with a label attached to his collar which read, 'I am a FIERCE guard dog, I will protect you.' And maybe he would, if the need arose. In the meanwhile he was company for her and he adored her.

He slept on her feet, and she was quite sure that she wouldn't sleep a wink tonight. She was prepared for tossing and turning, and was astounded next morning to realise that she must have dropped off almost as soon as her head touched the pillow ...

It was bad luck that she should be in the office with Neil when Coll rang her that afternoon. Often Neil had clients in and Dora was in the outer office, but at that time they were both there, and nobody else was, and Neil simply sat and listened from the moment Dora said, 'Oh, it's you.'

'Who's you?' said Neil's expression, and she should have explained, but her whole attention was riveted because Coll was telling her, 'It's all settled—the Manor.'

'Settled?' she shrilled. 'Do you mean you've actually bought the house since you saw it yesterday?'

'Yes. I've been in touch with Simon, and I'll see you both on Sunday afternoon.'

'See us where?'

'At the Manor. Where else?' He rang off while she was stammering, and she took the phone from her ear and held it helplessly as though she didn't know what to do with it.

'See you where?' asked Neil.

'At the Manor,' said Dora, and slammed the phone down.

'He doesn't waste much time,' observed Neil. 'Who are you calling now?'

'John Redway,' she said, picking up the phone again. 'Is it really settled?' she asked when she got through, and she was assured that it was.

The surveyors had arrived early this morning and the conveyancing was proceeding at a record-breaking rate. 'The man moves, doesn't he?' said the estate agent happily. 'Mrs Wardour can't believe her luck.' She was the woman who had owned the Manor. 'She thought she'd got a white elephant on her hands there.' He chuckled. 'And she had. The Manor isn't the only barny old house we've got on our books, if you'll pardon the expression. I thought we'd have to come down a fair bit in price and even then it could have hung on for years. She couldn't believe it when I rang her at her daughter's and told her.'

'I'm glad she's happy,' said Dora.

'We're all happy,' chortled John Redway. He was very cock-a-hoop, and it was as well he couldn't see Dora's face. Neither could Neil, she had her back to him. 'You know,' John went on, 'I believe it was meeting you and Simon again that tipped the balance.'

'Why, for goodness' sake?' asked Dora.

'Well, you knew each other as kids, didn't you? He said he used to come down to your village years ago.'

'He did,' she said.

Last night he had acted as though there were only happy memories, but the last time he saw Dora before that he had said, 'You stupid over-protected little slag, it's time somebody took something away from you.'

He had meant the pearls, but was he enjoying taking the Manor now? It might just have tipped the balance that the Holcrofts were still here—Simon, for whom his audacity and vagabond ways had been a glorious romp during a few brief boyhood hours, and Dora who had never liked him.

He might be genuinely pleased at the idea of Simon as a neighbour, their changed status could appeal to his ego. And he might be considering Dora an amusing challenge; he had been laughing at her last night when he kissed her.

But it was a sour joke. If he thought his money would bring her to heel he was very much mistaken. She wouldn't be patronised by a jumped-up con-man who had started as a small time thief.

She said, 'I'm glad we helped to get the old barn off your hands.'

'Did I say that? It's a fine old Georgian house.'

She laughed. 'Come off it! It's an old barn. Wait till he gets the heating bills.'

Although heating bills shouldn't worry a man who was almost a millionaire, nor one who had spent all his childhood sleeping in a battered trailer or under the stars. She said, 'I don't suppose he feels the cold,' and while the estate agent was inquiring, 'No, why not?' she hung up.

'Am I invited to the Manor?' asked Neil.

'What?' Dora turned with furrowed brow. 'Oh, I'm sure you will be, but that was for Sunday afternoon and there isn't likely to be much doing there on Sunday afternoon. I think we'll give that invitation a miss.'

Simon wasn't too pleased she wasn't going. He rang

her too at work to ask if she'd heard the news. 'I expect so,' she said.

'Coll's bought——'

'Yes, I've heard.'

'He wants us——'

'I know that too. Look, I'm busy now, I'll see you this evening.'

She called in the shop before she went home after work and found both Simon and Thea overjoyed. She'd expected that, but she couldn't help saying to Simon, 'You're carrying on as though it was our house again. It isn't, you know, and it never will be.'

'Stating the obvious, aren't you?' Simon was polishing up a chiffonier in the little workshop behind the shop, and Thea, who had come down when she heard Dora's car, was bouncing Kiki in her arms. Kiki wanted to get down and crawl, and the flagstoned floor wasn't over-hygienic. 'But if somebody else had to get it I'm glad it's Coll,' said Simon.

'Why?' demanded Dora, and Simon slapped down his polisher in exasperation.

'Because he likes us, doesn't he? We like him. He'll do the old place proud, and it's the next best thing to having it, isn't it, having the run of it?'

'I suppose so,' she agreed grudgingly, 'but you're carrying on as though our long-lost brother's come home.'

'Oh, don't act so wet,' said Simon. 'We're meeting him there on Sunday afternoon.'

'Not me.'

He sighed, rolling his eyes at Thea, appealing for her support, and Thea said mildly, 'I'm sure it doesn't matter if you've got something else fixed up. He did say if we could manage it he'd be there and he'd like to see us and perhaps we could have a meal together. I'm sure he's not going to take offence if Dora can't make it. He's not going to think it's personal.'

She swung Kiki towards Dora and the baby held out dimpled arms, chattering in unintelligible baby tongue. Dora took her and nuzzled nose to nose, and Kiki gurgled and dribbled with delight.

Simon, polishing hard, muttered, 'A pity he isn't our long-lost something. We could do with a relation like him.'

'Come and have a cup of tea,' said Thea, leading the way upstairs to the flat, leaving Simon still polishing.

She thought she understood. She thought that Dora was hating losing her old home a second time, resenting anyone who moved in, and that probably did have something to do with it. A cup of tea later Dora was saying, 'It's going to take some getting used to, him in the Manor, but they say you can get used to anything in time.'

'You got used to it being a hotel full of strangers,' Thea pointed out.

'Mmm.' But it was less the house than the man that was worrying Dora. How long was it going to take her to get used to him?

On Sunday she went to Neil's home to tea. There were places she would rather have gone, Mrs Hewitt was always a strain, and today she was full of the news about the sale of the Manor.

Everybody local knew by now, and that Coll had been a tinker child in his day and was now rolling in money. It was a rags to riches story, and although very few could remember him it had the makings of a good gossip.

Mrs Hewitt, presiding over her usual elegant Sunday tea-table, wanted to know just what was Dora's connection with this man. Neil must have been regaling her on Simon's reminiscences, but she wanted to hear for herself.

'You and your brother used to play with him, did you, when you were children?'

'Yes,' said Dora, sipping China tea from a beautiful china cup.

'I always feel sorry for the children,' said Mrs Hewitt sanctimoniously, 'but I never let Neil mix with them.' She sipped her tea, looking smug. 'But then of course you didn't have a mother, did you, dear, and your poor father was such an easy-going man.'

So easy-going that he'd got through a sizeable estate before he died of a coronary in his mid-forties. But Dora had loved him very much and she resented Mrs Hewitt's tone of voice. She said sweetly, 'Perhaps my father wasn't too bad a judge of character. After all, Coll has made more headway than anyone else we knew in those days, and it's nice that he still remembers us.'

Mrs Hewitt's lips thinned and Dora wished she could have recalled her words. That wasn't a tactful thing to say to Neil and his mother.

'He's a bachelor, I hear,' said Mrs Hewitt, as if that was highly suspect, although so was Neil, and she had always been happy about his single state. 'And I suppose you'll be seeing quite a lot of him while you're living in the lodge.'

'I don't know,' said Dora. Mrs Hewitt was doing this deliberately, and the thought crossed Dora's mind, not for the first time, that it would be a rare girl who would be happy with Mrs Hewitt as a mother-in-law.

All through tea Mrs Hewitt wouldn't let the subject of the new owner of the Manor alone. No matter how Dora tried to talk about something else, and Neil made a few half-hearted attempts, Mrs Hewitt came right back to Coll Sullivan, worrying away until Dora could have hit her.

And Neil too. Mrs Hewitt simply brushed his words aside and, apart from smiling apologetically at Dora, he let her go on with her endless insinuations as though it was all right and a pleasant enough way of passing a Sunday afternoon.

Perhaps he was curious too, but there was nothing Dora had to tell him that he hadn't heard already from Simon.

The phone rang and Neil went to answer it, and Mrs Hewitt leaned confidentially forward over the plate of neatly cut salmon and cucumber sandwiches she had been offering Dora.

'No, thank you,' said Dora, to another sandwich.

'Do you mind if I give you some advice, dear?' said Mrs Hewitt.

'Feel free.' Dora was feeling uncomfortable and embarrassed; she was pretty sure what advice she was going to get.

Mrs Hewitt, still holding her plate of sandwiches, said solemnly, 'Don't get carried away by this man. It might be flattering if he starts paying you attention, but you know that you'd only be one of many——'

'This isn't necessary,' said Dora, angry colour in her cheeks, and Mrs Hewitt smiled with a grim archness.

'I only hope it isn't. I only hope you'll remember

you're engaged to my boy, but you have changed your mind before, haven't you?'

It won't be your fault if I don't change it again, thought Dora, and tried to remember how nice Neil was, what a considerate employer, how reliable and kind. But any minute now she was going to have words with his mother, and it was by no means certain that Neil would take Dora's side.

He came back into the room in the nick of time and told her, 'That was your brother,' and as she jumped up thankfully, 'He's rung off.'

'What did he want?' she asked.

'He wants us to go round to the Manor.'

'Is that all he said?'

'No. He said they were all there, Thea and what's-his-name, and they were looking over the place and discussing it, and they wanted you along. Do you want to go?'

If it was a choice of going or staying here—yes, she did. 'Why not?' she shrugged.

'Of course my opinion doesn't matter,' said Mrs Hewitt, the acid swamping her surgery tones, 'but I shouldn't have thought that the Manor was Dora's business any more. Why should he want you there, Dora? Or your brother, come to that. Simon doesn't have any share in it, does he? Everybody knows that Simon and Thea are poor as church mice.'

'Perhaps Simon's tossed Coll for it and won,' said Dora. 'Perhaps Coll's a gambling man.'

'Like your poor father,' said Mrs Hewitt with a sigh.

Unfortunately it was true. Laurence Holcroft had lost, on the horses and the Stock Exchange, which was why Dora had been an idiot to give Mrs Hewitt that opening and showed she wasn't thinking too clearly.

As they got into the car Neil said, 'Mother's right.'

'Every time,' Dora muttered, 'but what are we talking about this time?'

'About the Manor not really being your concern any more.' That was playing on Neil's mind, he was frowning as he thought about it, asking her, 'Why should he want to involve you and Simon? What's he hoping to get out of that?'

'I cannot imagine,' said Dora.

'I saw the way he looked at you.' Neil was scowling at the road ahead and Dora shrugged, because Coll had hardly looked at her at all.

She said slowly, hoping this would sink in, 'He and Simon got on well enough as boys, the little they saw of each other, but I never liked him, and believe it or not I still don't like him.'

In profile Neil's mouth was downturned and sceptical. 'He'd even got a pet name for you,' he said. 'Dora-Lily. I've never heard anyone else call you that.'

He sounded hurt and she thought wildly—you've never heard anyone else call me a stupid little slag either. She said, 'That was no pet name. I don't like the name Lilias, I'm not crazy about Dora, but both together used to really rile me when I was a kid.'

'He'd remembered,' said Neil, as though that proved his point.

'Oh, forget it,' said Dora. 'Why are we going to the Manor anyway? Let's go somewhere else. How about Savernake Forest? Let's take a nature ramble.'

'They're expecting us at the Manor,' said Neil stubbornly, and Dora realised that he was going to watch her with Coll Sullivan, waiting for signs of intimacy. He was suspicious, very suspicious, of this man he considered a rival. 'I'd rather be around when you meet him,' he said, and she snapped,

'I'm not likely to be dating him alone, but if he suggests it I'll let you know.'

'So I should hope,' said Neil.

They drove to the Manor in silence. Dora did not want to go. If only Neil had agreed with her that it was a bore and unnecessary they could have gone off somewhere else and had a carefree hour or two. She had told him she disliked Coll, why couldn't he believe her, instead of playing the heavy fiancé?

She was sorry he was jealous. It was ridiculous. It irritated her, and it wasn't likely to be giving him any pleasure. He looked like a sulky boy. He was a solidly built man of middle height, and he had been a plump boy. 'My boy,' his mother still called him, and Dora's irritation evaporated because suddenly she could see what his mother meant.

She squeezed his arm and smiled. 'Cheer up,' she said, and he gave her a slight smile.

When they sold the Manor they had kept the lodge, and Dora had gone to live with Mrs Drayton who had lived in the lodge for the last forty odd years.

Thea had wanted Dora with herself and Simon at the shop, but even at seventeen, Dora was practical and romantic enough to feel that the newlyweds should be alone. She had always been fond of old Mrs Drayton and it was a convenient arrangement, the strong young girl helping the ailing old woman; Mrs Drayton giving devoted affection and stability. They were like grandmother and granddaughter, and Dora had been brokenhearted when she'd died just over four years ago.

She had resisted fresh offers then to move into the

flat over the shop. At twenty-two she preferred her own little home, and Thea and Simon had to settle for providing her with her small guard dog.

But they could hardly have been a closer family if Dora had been living with them. Thea had no other relations, and she and Dora were sisters in every sense.

Perhaps part of Dora hadn't wanted to leave the Manor altogether when she had decided she would like to go and live with Granny Drayton in the lodge. She had never walked up the drive again, until John took them to look over the empty house last month. She had rarely glanced in its direction, but she had always known it was there, behind the trees, and perhaps she had felt she was the watcher at the gate.

She almost held her breath now, driving between the cut grass verges that were beginning to straggle, the bushes that needed pruning, and the trees. The front of the house hadn't changed at all. It was perfectly proportioned Georgian, the pale grey Bath stone darkened by age, curtains still at the windows.

As they drew up the front door opened and Coll stepped out, and if she had been at the wheel she would have turned the car and driven away fast. She licked her dry lips and got out of the car on shaky legs.

Thea and Simon appeared almost immediately, or she doubted if she would have managed to walk up the steps towards the open door with Coll Sullivan framed in it. Every nerve in her body revolted against going through that door and being shown around her home, hers and Simon's, by the new master here.

But Thea and Simon were smiling, and Tip came rushing between feet, and she stooped to pat the small dog.

When they had walked around with the estate agent she had had hardly a pang. It had been like visiting a place where you had been happy but on which you no longer had any claims. Pretending they might buy it had been part of a game and she wouldn't have resented any other owner.

But she had always resented Coll, from the day he dropped out of the skies into the five-acre meadow. A farmer had bought the meadow when everything went up for sale. Pigs and sheep grazed between the walnut trees now, and it was hard to reconcile this man in the superbly cut suit with the skinny boy in ragged clothes.

But she resented him still. She could feel the same seething distrust and she moved away from him, into the hall.

It was an hotel foyer now, complete with reception counter. 'What are we here for?' she asked. 'A housewarming or another conducted tour?'

'A conducted tour, sort of,' said Simon. 'Coll wants us to put it back.'

'Put what back?' She jerked her head towards him, her body stayed rigid, and her eyes glittered as she repressed a desire to say, 'If we're putting things back how about starting with my pearls?'

'The house,' said Coll.

'The clock,' said Thea gaily. 'He wants it furnished more or less as it used to be.'

'Why?'

'It was mostly in period as I remember,' said Coll. His smile was slow and easy and self-mocking. 'From what I remember of what I saw. At the time I wasn't an expert on Georgian furniture.'

'You are now, of course?'

'Yes.'

'There was some Victorian,' said Simon.

A heavy carved sideboard was still here. A few pieces had gone with the first sale of the house, furniture that was not out of place for the Manor's role as a guest-house.

Almost everything else had been sold through the antique shop, but now they were going to put back the clock.

Once the contents of the Manor had been worth a small fortune, but in later years their father had begun selling off the valuable pieces. Both Simon and Dora had appreciated that he needed the money, although they had had no idea how deeply he was in debt until the bills were totted up after his death.

'You can't turn the clock back,' said Dora, and Simon chimed in with cheerful confidence,

'Rubbish, we're doing it all the time. Everything we sell brings back the past, the farther back the pricier. Come on now—in here. What did we used to have in here? A grandfather clock and what else?'

Simon knew as well as Dora did, and as she gazed around someone touched her arm. She had pulled away before she realised it was Neil, and that Coll hadn't moved. 'Can't you remember?' Coll asked her, voice grave, eyes mocking.

'Well enough,' she said, 'but I still don't understand why you want to reconstruct this house how it used to be. Don't you have any ideas of your own?'

'I've never been short of ideas,' he drawled, 'so put this down to a whim. I can afford whims.'

'Some whim,' she said shortly, 'but hooray for you. Is it a shopping list we're making out?'

'That's it.'

Some list! She resented the fact that he could order what he wanted on this scale. It was hard to swallow her envy and pretend to joke. 'You're sure you are nearly a millionaire? I shouldn't like you to end up as the second bankrupt in this house.'

Her father had not gone bankrupt, but he would have done if he had lived even another month or two. One of the bitter things about his death was hearing people saying he had been lucky to die.

'Wouldn't you?' He had white teeth and an attractive smile. He knew it was an attractive smile, just as he knew that she wouldn't care what happened to him. His eyes had no part in his smile as he took her hand, holding it as though he was reassuring her, 'Don't worry, I know what I'm doing.'

It was like a childish uneven trial of strength, only her whitened knuckles showed that she was trying to pull her hand from his encircling fingers. She smiled too, gritting her teeth. 'I'm glad to hear that. You'll have to settle for reproductions in some cases, of course, there aren't that many antiques going all at once. You can't order them like a load of bricks.'

'I appreciate that. We'll settle for reproductions until we can get the genuine articles.'

'*We?*' She was mocking too. 'Are you speaking as royalty, or are we in this together?'

He smiled at Thea and Simon, and asked, 'What do you think?'

'Of course we are,' said Simon, and Coll loosed her hand and she wanted to rub it because that grip had hurt, but she wasn't going to show anyone that it had hurt.

'We're not doing this for love, are we?' she said lightly. 'Simon and Thea will get their commissions?'

'A business deal, of course,' Coll assured them all. 'Not a love affair.'

'Then that's all right,' said Dora. 'Where do we start?'

An assignment like this would be a godsend. Often Simon and Thea were asked to keep an eye open for a particular article, but they had never been given carte blanche on anything like this scale. Simon would enjoy buying for the Manor because he had loved the old house.

They went from room to room, Thea taking notes as they discussed the kind of furniture that used to be here, the articles that Simon might be able to secure.

Most of the hotel furniture was still in place. The dining room was filled with small round tables and mock Regency chairs. The glass-fronted library shelves were locked and stocked with books that had been there from Dora and Simon's day—nothing of value, but some of them attractively bound. There were a couple of rows of Victorian novels that Dora had read as a young girl ... *Only a Child Bride, The Wayward Ward* ... She wondered if anyone had opened them since she closed them, and doubted it.

'I should keep a couple of the armchairs,' Simon was saying, and Dora stood quiet and calm, wondering why it had seemed so different when the estate agent had brought them round. Perhaps it was because now they were going back in much greater detail that she couldn't stop thinking of her father.

He had been a big man, always cheerful, which was strange when you knew that he must have been worried crazy towards the end. Or perhaps he wasn't. Perhaps he'd believed it would still turn out all right.

He *was* easy-going. Nothing had ever really seemed to bother him.

She missed him still, his big laugh, his bear hug, and sometimes she moved on ahead of the others, as though she might find him yet in some room behind some closed door.

The task took time. The bedrooms were hotel bedrooms, attractive if impersonal, and most of those could be left more or less as they were for the present. But Simon and Thea went into every room, taking notes, scribbling down suggestions.

Dora stayed by the window, in the bedroom she had always had, watching the dusk creep over the skies, until Tip curled up and slept at her feet.

When Thea came searching for her to say they were about to sit down and eat she asked, 'Where is everyone?'

'In the kitchen now,' said Thea. 'Simon and I have just finished up here. Coll and Neil are downstairs—I thought you were with them.'

'No,' said Dora unnecessarily, and Thea gave her a quizzical look.

'I wonder what they're finding to talk about.'

'I can't imagine,' shrugged Dora.

'Can't you?' said Thea.

Kiki, who had been sleeping in her carrycot on the kitchen floor, had woken when the kitchen was filled with activity. But she woke happy and was trying to bite on a rusk and chattering nineteen to the dozen.

There was a food basket on the table, picnic fare on a grand scale, and they sat down to a cutting of pies and quiches, and the soft plop of wine corks.

'This room's changed a bit, hasn't it?' said Simon. It was equipped as an hotel kitchen, with big white cookers and sinks and a microwave oven. There was nothing here of their childhood, except the view through the window where moonlight slanted on the stable block, and that was mostly garages now.

Dora didn't usually spend much of her waking life dreaming, but this evening had been a dreaming time. She was still doing it, remembering Folly, and the other horses, and the way the kitchen used to be.

She couldn't stop thinking about her father, and although the food was delicious she hardly ate anything. She put her wineglass to her lips several times and set it down almost untasted.

When Neil said they should be going she didn't hear him at first, and then she said, 'Yes, yes, of course,' coming out of her reverie blinking.

'Thank you for the supper,' she said to Coll.

'Any time,' he said.

He and Simon and Thea were still discussing what was needed for the house. Thea was nursing Kiki, who had dropped off to sleep again, and Thea and Simon showed no signs of moving.

When Dora got up so did Coll, although there was no need to see her to the door, she surely knew the way. But he went through the hall with them, and watched them get into the car with Tip, and Dora made herself turn because she had to get used to him in that doorway.

She hoped he would have closed the door and gone back into the house, but he hadn't. He didn't wave or move, he just stood there.

'I could have walked this, couldn't I?' she said, chattering nervously. 'I didn't need a lift for this little way. Are you coming in?'

'I am,' said Neil grimly.

'Oh! Oh, well yes, fine.'

She turned on the light and her living room was tiny after the spaciousness of the Manor. The walls seemed to close in on her, or perhaps it was Neil crowding her, breathing hard and scowling.

He said, 'It can't go on, you know.'

'What can't?'

'You know what I mean.'

'I don't.'

'You do.'

This was developing into one of those lunatic exchanges that were wasted breath, so she said, 'You'd rather I kept away from the Manor?'

'I'd rather you kept away from him.'

'All right.' That was easy enough to promise, that was what she intended to do. She sat down, suddenly exhausted, and Neil said querulously,

'You've been mooning over him all night.'

'Over Coll Sullivan?' That produced a weary smile. 'Don't talk rot,' she said. 'If you must know I've been thinking about my father. Being up there again brought back a few memories.'

'I don't believe you.' She waited for him to add, 'Do you take me for a fool?' and sure enough he did.

She said, 'If you don't believe me there isn't much I can do about it, is there?'

Neil was very stiff, his lips set in that rather childish pout. 'Now, Dora, I'm not going to stand for it. You're not going to treat me like you did the last two.'

That was excusable if not kind. It seemed that her past mistakes rankled with him, although he had never brought them up before.

He waggled a finger at her and she was reminded of his mother, leaning over the cucumber sandwiches this afternoon to give her a piece of free advice.

'But before you do start playing around again,' said Neil severely, 'let me remind you that you're not getting any younger.'

Dora's lips twitched. He was four years older than she was and she had no worries about her looks. She said sweetly, 'Who is? Although—I don't know, you're a bit of a Peter Pan. Maybe you should grow up.'

He coloured at that. He hadn't expected her to retaliate. He said, 'Mother said this was going to happen. Last night when I told her she told me—"Watch Dora".'

'I'll bet she did.' She was both angry and sad, and she wanted it over and she wanted him gone.

He was telling her, 'I don't want the kind of wife I've got to watch, so you'd better understand——' and she cut in,

'That you're my last chance and my roving days are over?'

'Yes.' He said it again, on an even firmer note. 'Yes,' and she took off her ring, picked up his hand, and slapped it on his palm.

'Present for you,' she said. 'Run home now.'

He stared down at the ring as though he had never seen it before; then, with tight shut lips, slipped it into his pocket. 'I'll talk to you in the morning.' His voice sounded tight too, as though he was holding in a lot of unpleasant thoughts.

Dora listened to the car and then she went back to the chair where she had been sitting, and sat down again looking at her hand without the ring. It wouldn't have worked. How could it? Mrs Hewitt would never have let it work.

And yet it might have done if she had stayed calm

and quiet and sensible, and Coll Sullivan had never come back.

He should have changed completely. The tinker-boy was a tycoon now, but he still had the knack of upsetting everything.

'The sun always seemed to be shining,' Simon had said, but she remembered that there were always clouds when Coll Sullivan was around, and crackle of thunder. There was always danger in the air.

He was not going to know that she had come straight from the Manor tonight, rowed with Neil and broken off her engagement, because that would have him laughing his head off. But not at her. She was giving him no excuse for laughing at her.

CHAPTER THREE

NOBODY in the office next morning noticed that Dora was not wearing her ring. She went on with her work and there was plenty to do, and Neil had several clients to see. After he had seen them he dictated some letters for Dora to type, and it was only when she took in the letters for signature just before lunch time that he said, 'About Coll Sullivan.'

She stayed uncompromisingly silent because she couldn't think what to say, and Neil, after a quick glance at the top letter which he couldn't fault—he rarely could fault Dora's work—demanded, 'Will you give me your solemn word to avoid him?'

She could have said, 'All right,' again because of course she would try to avoid Coll, but how was she going to satisfy Neil and his mother on that? He was deadly serious, and if Simon and Thea were getting furniture for the Manor there would be times when Dora would be going up there, and each time would mean an inquisition. She couldn't win. They wouldn't believe her so she couldn't win.

'No,' she said.

'I see,' said Neil.

'I don't think you do, but if you have to ask for a promise like that there's something very wrong with our relationship.'

'Oh Dora,' he sighed. 'Dora, Dora.' He shook his head at her. The old cliché 'More in sorrow than anger' summed it up, and she could imagine Neil and Mrs Hewitt shaking their heads together tonight over their evening meal, bewailing her ingratitude and her flighty nature.

There was really nothing funny about it, and if she had loved Neil deeply she would have been desperate. She *was* miserable, because although she had gone into this engagement with a cool head she was very fond of him and she had wanted to marry him.

But she couldn't now. Even if she promised everything he asked there would be a probationary period, during which Mrs Hewitt would see her off for some reason or other, with Coll Sullivan as odds-on favourite.

Neil left it at that. He went, with no suggestion that she might join him for lunch, as she usually did, and he was out of the office all afternoon. She didn't see him again before she finished work for the day; and when she got back to the village she called at the shop, which had just closed, to tell Thea all about it.

Simon had gone rounding up several pieces they thought might be suitable for the Manor. He had phoned some fellow dealers this morning, describing what he was after, and he had gone to look at, and possibly return with, what they had to offer.

Thea had the evening meal almost ready, and laid another place for Dora while she was hearing that Dora had handed back her ring last night because Neil had accused her of mooning over Coll, and warned her that at her age she should be considering him, Neil, as her last chance.

'He's potty,' said Thea cheerfully.

'He's jealous,' said Dora. 'His mother doesn't think I've got a good record, having been engaged twice before. She warned me to remember I was engaged to her boy before we came over last night, and this morning I think Neil wanted a signed affidavit that I'd keep right away from Coll Sullivan.'

Thea laughed. 'They're both potty. Simon will laugh. Do you mind very much?'

'Well,' Dora was down on her knees, building up bricks on the lino that Kiki knocked flying as soon as the stack was high enough to make a satisfying clatter, 'better to find out now that we're not suited than wait until we were married.'

'Much better,' agreed Thea. 'Will you look for another job?'

'I might have to.'

'At least you can do that.' Thea sat down at the table, chin in her hands. 'The shop's our living and we're stuck with it.' She sounded wistful. Thea was usually very contented, but Coll Sullivan had probably unsettled them all.

Although Simon had been pleased to see Coll again he must be sensitive about the extent that life had changed for both of them. The boy who had had nothing had so much now, while the Holcrofts—as Mrs Hewitt had pointed out—were poor as church mice.

Simon didn't seem to care, but both he and Thea must be wondering where all his advantages of birth had got him, while Coll Sullivan could buy the Manor as though he was paying for a packet of peanuts.

Dora put another brick very carefully on top of her tower of four and said, 'Coll Sullivan started with a natural advantage for getting on these days. He's quite unscrupulous.'

Thea didn't ask what childish memories Dora was basing that on. 'I should think he is,' she said. 'But he must be clever and he must be lucky.'

Dora turned over the brick in her hand, studying the picture of a rabbit, 'B' for Bunny. 'You took to him, didn't you?'

'He's attractive,' said Thea. 'Anybody can see that. And if we're finding most of his furniture for him that's marvellous. Simon was hoping he'd come back with something worthwhile today.'

'To put the house in order for Coll?'

'Why not?' Thea pushed back her heavy dark hair, that she wore in a fringe and falling loose. She usually wore long skirts, and today's dress was a cotton print of small pale blue flowers on a dark blue ground. Dora was in a beige shirtwaister, Neil liked discreet clothes at work. He liked discretion in most things.

Thea was talking about Coll, who had been dressed discreetly too, in an expensive immaculate suit, and yet had generated a fierce disruptive alchemy.

She was saying, 'Why not? He said last night that he'd been thinking for some time of moving into a house, and when he saw the Manor advertised in the

Sunday Times he thought he'd come down and have a look at it.'

Kiki sent the tower tumbling, and Dora began building it up again automatically, most of her attention with Thea. All this talking must have been done after she and Neil had left. How long did they stay, she wondered, sitting around the kitchen table?

Thea was smiling, as though this was a nice story. 'When he saw it again he realised that it used to be part of a boyhood dream he'd forgotten, but it was still the kind of house he wanted, and finding you and Simon here was—well——' words seemed to fail her. 'Incredible.'

'Why should it be incredible?' asked Dora. 'There are Holcrofts in the churchyard who've been there for three hundred years.' That was flippant, and Thea said with the faintest note of reproach,

'He was always being moved on when he was a boy so he might not appreciate how secure some families are.'

Dora smiled, 'And it's nothing to be proud of, is it? We just lacked get-up-and-go. From the Manor to the churchyard, and nice cushy lives in between. But it's a very different world these days.'

She picked up Kiki and lifted her eye-to-eye height. 'And as for you my pet, the last of the Holcrofts, if you ever have a birthday party in the Manor it will be by courtesy of the boy who pushed Arnold Rigby's face in the trifle when he came to my party.'

'Who was Arnold Rigby?' Thea asked, smiling, and Dora kissed Kiki's nose.

'A nice little boy, but his parents never let him come to another party at our house.'

Boys fighting at a birthday party was a natural

hazard of youthful high spirits, but she was tempted to confide in Thea about her pearls, because that had a different feel to it. That was nasty. Coll had been a young man then, light-fingered and untrustworthy, and who was to say that he could be trusted now?

'Prove it,' he had said. She couldn't prove it then, and she couldn't prove it now, but now he was the rich man and they had nothing he would want to steal, so perhaps it didn't matter whether he could be trusted or not.

It would only stir up trouble, put a blight on what must be a profitable business arrangement for Thea and Simon. So she said nothing.

She began to build again with the wooden bricks, but when she set Kiki down the baby crawled off to start a tug of war with Tip over a battered teddy bear.

Simon had a fair day's haul. He brought along several chairs, a corner cupboard and a small table for Coll's approval; and a list of other possibles. He was keen on getting along to the Manor and seeing what they could do with the drawing room. Coll was due back about nine o'clock and Simon and Thea were meeting him there.

'You'll come, won't you?' Thea said to Dora, who swallowed her mouthful of steak and kidney pie—they were eating the evening meal—and said,

'I don't think so, thanks.'

'Scared what Mrs Hewitt would say?' Thea teased, and Simon asked,

'What's it got to do with mother-in-law?'

Thea waited to see if Dora was going to explain. Simon hadn't noticed she wasn't wearing her ring, folk really were very unobservant, but Dora wasn't going into details right now. He'd be less understanding than Thea. He'd think it was a great joke, and it was likely he'd relate it to Coll at the first opportunity.

'Oh, very well,' she said, 'but it's a bit of an effort for me.' She tried to smile. 'The old place, you know. It was different when we were walking round with John Redway, I didn't mind then, but last night——'

Her lashes were suddenly wet and she made a small grimace.

'I do know,' said Simon. 'I'm sorry.' Dora's wide grey eyes, so like his own, widened even more, and he said huskily, 'In the last ten years I should have made enough to get it back for you both.'

Thea made a soft little murmur of protest and re-assurance, and Dora said, 'I didn't mean that. Even if we got it back what could we do with it? It isn't suit-able for us any more. The upkeep will cost a fortune.'

'Coll Sullivan's made a fortune,' said Simon. He pushed aside his plate as though he was losing his appetite. 'And he'll he a millionaire before he's through. He'll get anything he sets his mind on. He always had to win.'

'But you liked him?' Thea asked anxiously, and Simon grinned.

'Of course I like him. He was a wild one, but we had some great times when he came. He'd take on any-thing. I used to feel that the sky was the limit when he was around. I used to wonder sometimes what hap-pened to him.'

'Did you?' said Dora. 'You never talked about him.'

'No, we never did, did we?' said Simon.

Perhaps that was because their lifes had changed so completely after that last time Coll came to the Manor. They didn't talk much about the past. It was bound up with the loss of their father and the loss of their world. The new life was Thea and the little antique shop, and Dora going to secretarial college, then taking jobs and acquiring boy-friends.

Until the estate agent told them who was buying their old home Dora couldn't remember Coll Sullivan's name ever being mentioned. But Simon had wondered about him.

Sometimes she had too. But when he had come into her mind she had put him out again. You don't linger over unpleasant memories and she had never liked him.

Thea stacked the plates. There was a good meal there for Tip, nobody seemed to have eaten up. Then she began to scoop out from a bowl of caramel cream. She said, 'He said the Manor was a boyhood dream, the kind of house he'd dreamed of living in, and now he's come back for it, and good luck to him. We don't want it, do we, Dora? Miles of floors, to scrub—no, thanks, and *how* many bedrooms?'

'Too many,' said Dora.

'I like my little flat,' confessed Thea. 'I like my little shop.' She put a dish of caramel in front of Simon. 'And I'd hate to be married to a millionaire.'

'No danger of that,' said Simon. 'I can't even keep out of the red.'

It was a joke tinged with wryness, and Dora stuck out her left hand, 'Notice anything?'

What did it matter if Simon thought it was funny, her engagement being broken off? He had always considered Neil a bit of a joke, and that should get his mind off money matters.

'Four fingers and a thumb,' said Simon. 'It looks much as it's always looked to me.'

'No ring,' said Thea.

'Has mother-in-law asked for it back?' Simon sounded ready to laugh, and Dora said,

'We had words, me and my ex-young-man.'

'My God, she's done it again,' said Simon. 'What was it about this time?'

'Nothing much. Mrs Hewitt thought we were going to live with her, and between them I saw rather a constricted future.'

'Well, there would be, wouldn't there?' said Simon. 'What are we going to do with her?' he asked Thea, and Thea put an arm around Dora.

'She's going to wait for the right man, like I did.'

Thea had been twenty when she'd married Simon, but at twenty-six Dora still had no real idea what kind of man she was waiting for. She had no dream ideal, no repeating pattern in the type that attracted her. Her two broken engagements before Neil had been dissimilar men, and Neil hadn't been much like either of them.

When the right man did come along, if he ever did, she only hoped she would recognise him.

Dusk was beginning to fall when they reached the Manor, and you might have imagined that time had stood still, except for the silence. There had always been a staff here in the old days, always movements somewhere, always light. The house had never stood still and silent and shadowed like this.

Simon opened the front door and turned on the hall lights, and Dora muttered, 'I suppose we should go round to the tradesmen's entrance.'

'Not us,' chortled Simon. 'We're friends of the master.'

'Don't call him that!' said Dora sharply and Simon said gently,

'It's a joke, love.'

But somehow, to her, it wasn't. The sound of it bothered her. The sound of it bothered her. Coll Sullivan had bought a house, no more. Simon and Thea were supplying him with goods, but he was master of nothing here except this house and its contents.

Thea touched Dora's arm and said, 'Give us a hand, getting the cot down.'

Dora needed something to do, and fast. She was standing like a zombie just inside the hall.

There was a cot upstairs in one of the bedrooms and Thea planned to put it in what had been the sewing room down here, so that while she was moving around on the ground floor Kiki would be secure and within earshot if they left doors open.

Thea never used a baby-sitter if she could help it. She would have been happy carrying her baby everywhere on her back. She was a born natural mother, and after waiting so long Kiki was her little miracle.

The girls manoeuvred the cot down. Doors and staircase were wide enough to get it through without dismantling it. And then the baby, still in her carrycot, was deposited inside, and Thea hovered over her singing a soft lullaby until she was sure that Kiki was deep in slumber.

In the meantime Simon had carted his pieces into the drawing room, and was trying them out here and there for effect.

The dog warned them that Coll was arriving, giving Simon time to get to the front door as the car drew up, with Dora frantically hushing Tip. 'You wake that baby,' she warned him, 'and I'll lock you in the cellars! This house has cellars. You've never been down a cellar, have you? One more yap and you're for it!'

Coll was brought straight into the drawing room, and Dora realised that they were all anxiously awaiting his approval. Simon and Thea looked quite worried, eyes on his face as he inspected the furniture that Simon hoped to buy on his behalf.

The prices were high although Simon was only asking a modest commission. The stuff was good, collectors' pieces, genuine antiques. When Simon quoted figures Dora knew that he was apprehensive, and her hold on Tip tightened so that the little dog squirmed and turned to look up at her.

'Fine,' said Coll, and Simon and Thea broke into smiles. They showed him everything in more detail then, pointing out the beauty of craftsmanship, assuring him that these were investments—which Dora was sure he knew anyway; and Simon began to tell him what else was available, producing the notes he had made on his travels today.

'Have you eaten?' Thea asked.

'Yes,' said Coll. 'Thank you.'

'Are you sure?'

He laughed then and admitted, 'Not recently.'

'I'd have brought something if I'd known.' Thea sighed at her own lack of foresight and Dora felt like saying, 'Why should you? Surely he's capable of feeding himself.'

Dora had said nothing since Coll walked in. He had neither spoken to her nor looked at her, and she remembered that too from their childhood. Now he managed to ignore her as though she wasn't there, or as though she didn't matter. She didn't matter in this transaction, she wasn't buying the furniture for him, nor getting his food, but a glance and a good evening would have been civil.

'Let's have a fire,' he said suddenly.

The big white marble fireplace stood empty. It was a warm night, they had opened a window in here, but the fireplace was the focal point of the room and, although the previous owners had installed central heating, fires had burned in the drawing room to cheer the hotel guests.

Neither Simon nor Thea were much good at fire-lighting, they had a gas fire in their living room, but there was an open grate in the lodge and Dora said, 'All right, I'll light one if I can find some kindling.'

There were a couple of logs left in the hearth, and a half filled brass coal scuttle, and there would probably be some sticks and paper down in the cellar.

'Yes,' said Simon hastily, 'well, I'll get phoning about this.' He held up his notebook, and Thea laughed,

'And I'll get a supper tray.'

'I wouldn't hear of you lighting the fire,' said Coll to Dora, with what sounded like courtesy. 'I will.'

She shrugged and went. She found some sticks and a newspaper that didn't seem too damp, and came back into the drawing room where twigs were crackling away in the hearth and Coll was feeding them slowly with small pieces of coal. The coal had caught, the fire was well away.

Dora stood back and looked at it, then dropped her small load in the hearth and said, 'That was quick.'

'I learned how to light a fire when I was very young,' he said, as though they were talking about playing chess, and she said shortly,

'I suppose you would, but I shouldn't think you've had much practise lately.'

He got up. He *was* tall, and it was an effort to stand

still and not move away. He had always threatened her peace of mind, but suddenly, although he was smiling, the threat seemed physical.

'Once learned never forgotten,' he said lightly. 'Like swimming. Or making love.'

She said, 'You could swim very well, I remember.' Down where the weir was, and it was dangerous, and Simon would have gone in too if Dora hadn't been in tears. Although perhaps Simon did have more sense. Coll seemed to take risks for their own sake, as though life had to have an edge on it.

'My repertoire has increased since then,' he said, and her gaze dropped from his face to his hands. The long strong fingers were black with coal dust. Lovemaking, he meant that he was adept at that too, and her mind registered shock at the thought of him making love. To her. Of herself touched, taken.

A rush of revulsion sent her stumbling back, seeing nothing, certainly not the footstool just behind her; so that she would have gone flying if he hadn't moved faster than she could think.

He caught her in his arms and held her until she croaked something, and when he let her go she went on croaking, looking at her shoulders where the coal dust lay and his hands had touched her.

He said laconically, 'It will wash off.'

It had all happened in seconds. Everything. Nothing. Nothing had happened except that she had stumbled and he had steadied her and there were marks on her dress.

'Yes, of course,' she said, but she was rubbing at the dust, frantically trying to shift it, and he drawled,

'Although you may need a bath to get rid of my contaminating touch.'

That was how she felt, and it was irrational, but she managed to laugh and say, 'What *do* you mean?'

She knelt down in front of the blaze and began to feed it with the sticks she had brought, and when Thea walked in a minute or two later she was still kneeling, her back to Coll.

'Food,' said Thea.

'I need to wash,' said Coll.

'So do I,' said Dora when he had left the room.

'Nice fire,' commented Thea.

'He lit it,' said Dora. 'He says it's a knack you never forget.'

She went to the kitchen, and stayed longer than she needed just to wash her hands. She stood at the sink, looking out at the stable block and trying to calm herself. She felt almost faint, as though she had been actually attacked, and she didn't want to go back into any room where Coll Sullivan was.

But she had to, and she had to get rid of this crazy idea that he threatened her. How could he?

They were all seated around the fire, Coll was eating from the tray of assorted leftovers that Thea had made look quite appetising, and Simon was talking about the changes locally in the last ten years.

As Dora walked in Coll looked across at her. 'Washed it off?' he asked quietly.

'Mmm.' She sat on a sofa beside Thea, and Simon went on with what he was saying.

The furniture had changed in here since the old days, but it was still the same room, and in the firelight Dora found herself slipping back again into a musing reverie.

Then Coll got up, and he was the host, offering drinks, pouring out, and that was nothing like the old days; and as she looked at him he asked, 'Do I seem out of place?'

He did to her, because she was remembering her father, but not to anyone who wasn't hooked on the past. He looked as though he owned the house, if that was what he meant, at home. 'I'm sure you can play any part you choose,' she said, and he smiled.

'I'd have done quite well as a repertory actor. I've got an Identikit face.'

She looked at him standing there, relaxed and elegant, the dark smooth hair springing back from a peak, the cleft chin. A smooth supercilious hawkish face, cool and well bred. That was how he looked.

'A mask of a face,' she said softly, and he took that up cheerfully.

'And very useful too. I wouldn't have got far if I hadn't been able to hide what I'm thinking.'

'Now you're making me nervous,' said Thea, pretending to shudder, and Coll turned to her, his voice sounding warm and sincere.

'I hope not. I prefer to do business with people who trust me.'

Thea smiled. 'But of course we trust you.'

He had signed a cheque for the articles that Simon had brought along tonight, and presumably for the house. And to have been handed the key just like that meant he had to be who he said he was. For a moment Dora had thought—suppose he *is* a confidence trickster, and regretfully had to discard the idea.

Coll said, 'That was a suspicious little gleam in your eyes,' and she frowned, annoyed at being read so easily, and said,

'I'll turn away next time. I'm not so good at hiding what I'm thinking.'

'And you don't entirely trust me?' The impudence of that took her aback. Before she could say, 'No, and with very good reason,' he said, 'A pity, because I was thinking we might do another business deal.'

'Like what?' she said, contemptuously.

He was talking to Simon and Thea. 'Your shop's leasehold.' It wasn't a question, but Simon said,

'Yes.'

'Do you want to buy the freehold?'

'We can't afford to,' said Thea.

'I could lend you the money.'

Dora felt as though a net was closing on them. She wanted to jump to her feet and break out, but Simon and Thea were looking at each other with a dawning hope.

'On what terms?' Dora demanded harshly, and Coll said in the amiable voice of a reasonable man,

'I should want collateral, of course.'

'Of course,' Dora muttered, and he went on, ignoring her,

'But I'd be prepared to improve the look of the place for you, and we could get together over the more pressing financial problems.'

He seemed to know more about the business than Dora did. She hadn't realised the problems were so pressing, but Simon's air of astonished relief was admitting it now.

'What kind of collateral?' Dora persisted. Simon and Thea looked in a state to agree to anything, but Coll Sullivan would want his pound of flesh, whether it was a share in the shop, or perhaps he wanted to buy the Lodge now that he had the Manor. Whatever it was the time to spell it out was now, before Simon and

Thea accepted this highly generous, highly suspect offer.

Simon grimaced. 'We don't have much that's worth much.'

'I wouldn't say that,' said Coll.

When he said nothing more Dora broke the silence; it was as though Thea and Simon were scared to. 'What, then? What would you consider as security?'

Thea and Simon wanted this backing. Thea, beside Dora, was leaning tensely forward, and two deep stress lines cut between Simon's brows.

This time Coll didn't look at either of them, but straight at Dora. He said softly, smiling, but under it all was a steeliness of purpose, 'You.'

CHAPTER FOUR

'HA-HA,' said Dora, 'very funny.' The silence was puzzled as Thea and Simon waited for an explanation, then Coll said,

'You're not wearing your engagement ring.'

She looked down at her hand and said drily, 'You're the first observant one I've met all day.' She wouldn't show how shaken she was. She would be cool, even a little amused at his presumption, whatever he was going to say next.

Simon said abruptly, 'Are you asking Dora to marry you?' and she had to deal with that, and fast. She laughed, on a harsh note,

'At the risk of repeating myself, very funny,' and Coll smiled.

'At the risk of sounding unchivalrous—hell, no. I'm offering her a job.'

She heard Simon and Thea relax, Thea's soft little 'Oh' and Simon's 'Ah' as though that was going to be all right, then.

'I take it the engagement is off,' said Coll.

'As it happens,' said Dora airily, 'yes.'

'And you'd feel awkward still working for the man?'

'Why should I?' She raised both eyebrows. 'We never did mix business with pleasure,' and Coll grinned again. He had very white teeth, very dark eyes, and she wished she could say, 'Stop grinning at me!'

'Having met Neil Hewitt I'm sure you didn't,' he said.

'Do you?' she asked.

'Not as a rule. This would be a hands-off arrangement.'

She wanted no arrangement, no connection with him whatever. The moment he had looked straight at her and said, 'You,' had hit her like a knife blow. She was sitting calmly, but inside she was screaming and running for cover.

Thea said, 'Dora's a first-class secretary.'

'Excellent,' said Coll. He didn't sound as though it surprised him, but it probably did. In the old days she had been trained for nothing, except perhaps a good marriage, which meant marriage to a rich man. He said, 'I'd like Dora around to help me get this house in order.'

She could do that, but she wouldn't, not for him; and Thea sounded doubtful now. 'You mean as a housekeeper?'

'Housekeeper-cum-secretary. There'll be domestic staff, of course.' He could offer good wages and there was very little employment going locally. He'd get domestic staff.

'Why me?' asked Dora coldly. 'Why do you want me around?'

Because she was a Holcroft and he fancied having the Holcrofts, late of the Manor, at his beck and call? He could hardly admit that, but what other reason could there be?

He was holding his glass, he hadn't drunk any since he'd poured it, but he took a sip now, and then he said, 'As a good luck charm, Dora-Lily. I think you'll bring me luck.'

She goggled, gulped and said, 'I think you must be out of your mind!'

'Not at all.' He leaned back in his chair, charming confident and confiding; and there had never been a man she distrusted more.

'They were lucky days for me down here,' he went on. 'The more I think about it the more I realise that a lot of my luck started with you.' He looked around the room. Sometimes he had come into the house with Simon, into this room. 'Maybe this place gave me a taste for high living. If I hadn't met you both I might have stayed a travelling man.'

That was nonsense. Envy might have spurred him on a little, but he was born to travel in style. She couldn't remember ever having seen his father, but Coll had every qualification for success. Particularly the unpleasant ones like ruthlessness, and a talent for using people. He had Thea and Simon jerking on strings now, like two puppets, and he wanted Dora twitching to his touch too.

Not if she could help it, but she had to get out of this without causing a scene that would show he was under her skin, as well as upsetting Thea and Simon.

He said softly, 'I took something away from here that—well, gave me my start, I suppose,' and only his curved lips smiled.

Her pearls! They hadn't been fabulous. Some of her mother's jewellery had been worth a great deal more, the real old family heirlooms that her father had sold. But he would have got something on them that could have gone towards that first dump he had bought, and renovated and sold.

He couldn't mean that! He couldn't have the nerve to be talking about her pearls!

But he was. He was challenging her, eyes glinting and with a mocking half smile. He wanted her to start babbling accusations so that he could cut her down. But if she did it wouldn't be in front of Simon and Thea, or anybody. If she settled accounts with Coll Sullivan it would be a very private matter.

She said, 'Get yourself a horseshoe. I'm no good luck charm.'

He sighed as though he was disappointed. 'No you, no deal,' he said. 'I told you I can afford whims. This is how I see this one.'

She wondered how many board meetings he had addressed in the same quiet fashion, wasting no words, expecting no arguments. 'I'll buy the freehold of the shop,' he said, 'and advance whatever Simon and Thea feel is necessary to get the business rolling. On condition that you stay in my employment for six months, acting as secretary if I need a secretary while I'm down here, helping to get this house habitable and helping to run it.'

Dora wondered if he wanted her around because she was unpredictable and might even be dangerous. He had been waiting for her to say something about the pearls. He knew she disliked him, he had always known that, and now she amused him and he was enjoying the conflict.

She took a deep slow breath and said, 'No.'

'A pity,' he said.

'Look,' said Simon, 'could we have a family confab about this?' and Coll got up.

'Of course. I'll take my drink into the library.'

Thea spoke first, perplexed because she couldn't understand why Dora was being so dogmatic. Thea thought Dora might have considered before she said 'No' so fast, when there seemed so many reasons why her answer should have been 'Yes.'

'You're a good secretary,' Thea said. 'And you could get this house into a private home again. We could help you with that.'

Simon said, 'Maybe he does feel you're lucky for him.'

'Bosh!' Dora snorted.

Thea suggested, 'Do you think he's feeling guilty about your engagement being broken off? He did have something to do with that, didn't he? Neil was jealous of him.'

That was news that came as no surprise, from Simon's expression. He had seated himself on the sofa now, so that Dora was between the two people she loved best, both seeing in her the answer to their problems.

Dora said grimly, 'I don't think his conscience ever bothers him. More likely it appeals to his ego to own our old home and have both of us working for him.'

'We've got to work for somebody.' Every line in Simon's handsome face seemed a little deeper, as though he was ten years older and still in debt.

Thea was studying Dora's face closely, trying to understand. 'Why don't you want to work for him?'

'Because I don't like him,' Dora burst out. 'I never did.'

'Why?' Thea persisted, but it wasn't easy to explain. She didn't trust him because he had stolen her pearls, but she had never liked him. It had been a gut reaction from when she was six years old, and that was rather too early to be claiming female intuition.

She said, 'I don't know. Life seemed pretty secure in those days, but he used to come without warning and while he was here nothing was the same. He—upset everything.' She floundered, looking helplessly from one to the other, and Simon snapped,

'But we weren't secure, were we? We only thought we were.' He jumped up suddenly and walked away from them, down the long room, talking without turning, 'And there's never been any security since, we'll be going bust unless we get some luck from somewhere.'

'Surely not,' said Dora. Simon often joked about living on credit, but Thea was biting her lip now, looking close to tears. 'You never said it was this bad.' Dora reached for Thea's hand, almost glaring at Simon's back, and Thea said,

'What's the use of moaning? And we're keeping our heads above water, there are lots worse off than we are. But this does sound like the best thing that's happened in years.' She looked as though it could be the answer to her prayers. 'To have the freehold of the place, there's always the worry what's going to happen when you don't own it; and if someone would invest some capital with us it would make all the difference. We never had any capital, you know, it's always been hand to mouth.'

'It would only be for six months.' Simon stood where he was, as though he felt that if he came any closer he would grab Dora and shake some sense into her. 'We'd be paying him back, of course, but I'm sure he'll give us reasonable terms on the condition that you work for him for six months, and it doesn't seem much to ask.'

Six months didn't sound very long, and probably Coll would be away most of the time, but she didn't want to do it. She desperately wanted to say 'No' again.

'I know you didn't get on all that well with him,' said Simon, who had never mentioned that before, 'but you were both kids then.'

Coll had never seemed a child, there had always been a self-sufficiency in him, and the gap between them was deeper than four years difference in age. He was almost the same age as Simon, but the difference was there too.

The last time he had been twenty and in appearance he hadn't changed much. His skin was still smooth, almost unlined. He was better dressed, of course, but his body hadn't softened. It was still hard and taut and she remembered being held against him a little while ago, when she had stumbled here in front of the fire. She pressed her lips with the back of her hand, as though someone had kissed her mouth and she was wiping it away.

Inside he was the same too, she would swear to that. 'He hasn't changed,' she said.

'Don't be so thick,' said Simon wearily. 'Of course he's changed. He owns the Manor now, he can give

Thea and me our first real chance. What's that if it's not a change?'

'Money,' said Dora. Coll Sullivan hadn't changed in any fundamental way.

'We're not selling you to the man.' Simon was losing his temper. 'He wants you to work for him, not sleep with him.'

'Simon,' said Thea sharply, 'that's not funny!'

'You're damn right it isn't,' Simon exploded. 'What's the fuss about? So Dora doesn't want to work for Coll and that's probably why he wants her to, because she was such a little bitch to him in the old days. But we can't afford our pride any more. We had hundreds of years being top-dog and now we're the peasants, mate, and he's the master, and for God's sake, Dora, we've got to face up to it.'

His flare of anger subsided. He was almost always a good-tempered man, he had his father's bonhomie. It was Dora who had been born with spirit and stubbornness. They looked enough alike to be twins, except that Simon was older, but Dora always realised that Simon's was the nicer nature.

He grinned at her now. 'You know you're going to do it,' he said.

'Under protest.' She smiled back, grimacing.

'Who tells him?' Simon asked.

'I do.' She took her pocket mirror and a tissue out of her handbag, and wiped off the lipstick she had smudged on her mouth. Then she replaced it with a fairly steady hand, combed her silky sun-streaked hair and asked, 'Do I look efficient?'

'Thank you,' said Thea, and Dora laughed

'Oh, it shouldn't be so bad once I get used to the

idea. I'm going to enjoy getting the house in order. I can always pretend it's for us.'

But that kind of daydreaming could hurt, so she must never risk it. She must always remember that this was Coll Sullivan's property.

'I hope he intends to pay me a decent wage,' she said. 'I'd better check whether he thinks he can charge me against the loan, because if he does he's got another think coming.'

He was standing in the library. There were armchairs around, but he was standing with a book in his hands and the glass door of one of the library shelves open. As Dora walked into the room he looked at her, heavy lidded and expressionless.

Her spine prickled and she lifted her chin a fraction higher and said, 'Simon tells me I've got to work for you.'

'Do you always do what Simon tells you?'

She watched Tip trot forward, tail wagging, and wished he was a less friendly dog. She would have preferred something that snarled, or even bit, when Coll Sullivan was near.

She followed the dog, seating herself. 'I don't do what anyone tells me unless the reasons are good,' she said quietly. 'Simon and Thea need the money.'

'I know.' He must have gone into their circumstances thoroughly. She wondered if files on the Holcrofts had been put on some enormous executive desk for him, or if a secretary had read out notes, and she resented both his power and his cheek. It was a cheek, making their private business his business.

'Of course you know,' she said shortly. 'Will it be an

ego-booster for you, ordering Simon and me around?'

'Do you think I need an ego-booster?'

He never had, not even when he was in ragged clothes. Now there was arrogance oozing out of him, the lift of the head, the curl of the mouth. He looked like Lord Byron, that was what he looked like. With a dash of Lucifer. He had all the confidence in the world, and she could have spat in his face.

She said, 'Put it another way. Will it amuse you?'

'Immensely.' He shut the book he had been holding, replaced it in its set, and closed the glass door of the bookcase. It was one of the Theatre of Molière, in French. Dora wondered if he read French, and realised it wouldn't surprise her if he did.

'You're not helping us out of the goodness of your heart, are you?' she said, and Coll smiled very slowly. In this smile there was a subtle difference that made her blood run cold.

Simon had just said she had always behaved badly to Coll. She had been a spoiled child, her father's favourite. She hadn't wanted the tinker-boy around, taking Simon away during those precious summer holidays. But the last time had been the worst, that must be what he was remembering now.

He had taken her pearls and she had asked if his father was in jail. She hadn't known his father was dead. None of them had known, but he had smiled at her then as he was smiling at her now, and said it was time someone took something away from her.

She had a feeling that the next six months were going to be grimmer than any previous period in her life. When their father died and the house had to go, and she and Simon had to pick up the pieces and start again, she had thought—I survived. After this I can face anything, because no other time can be as bleak or as heartbreaking.

She had been heartbroken then, but she had never been as apprehensive as she was now, with this iron band around her throat and every nerve in her body tightening. She knew that she should be wary of what this man had in store for her, and she said, 'The job will be no joyride, will it?'

'Don't you think you can take it?'

'I can take anything you can hand out.' If he had some warped idea of bettering her, bullying her, he would find he was up against more than he'd bargained for.

'We'll see, won't we?' he said, and she nodded as though that was all quite satisfactory.

'I'll have to hand in my notice and work out the month, but in the meantime I could come up here evenings and weekends.'

'Excellent. What salary are you getting now?'

She told him, and he quoted a higher figure. She wished he hadn't, because it showed how little her salary meant to him. She wished he couldn't have afforded her, and she asked, 'Do you think I'm going to be worth that much?'

'You'll be worth it,' he drawled. 'When you're around I appreciate my luck.'

The contrast, he meant, remembering how things used to be, comparing with how they were today, knowing that the girl who had called him 'scum' was on his staff and paid to serve him.

That would be fine for his pride, but not so good for hers or Simon's, and she said bitterly, 'You knew I never liked you.'

'Of course.' He shrugged it off, it didn't matter.

'You never liked me either.' He didn't trouble to deny it. 'Mutual dislike isn't much of a basis for a working partnership,' she said.

His dark eyebrows rose. 'Who said anything about a partnership. While I pay the wages I give the orders,' and she had to swallow her resentment.

She patted the little dog who was sitting on the floor beside her chair, giving her voice time to get back to normal. Then she said, 'You whistle and I come?'

'That about sums it up.'

'When do you aim to start whistling?'

'You'll know when I do.'

She was about to snap, 'You won't get me running to heel,' when the door opened on a worried-looking Simon trying to look cheerful.

'Any hitches?' he asked, and Coll smiled at Dora.

'None. We understand each other.'

'We always did,' said Dora.

That didn't really reassure Simon, but if everything appeared to be all right he wasn't going to dig beneath the surface. They were both smiling and Coll had said there were no hitches. Simon's reaction was to get down to the business talk as quickly as possible.

His future, and Thea's and Kiki's, was at stake here. Coll could help them all to a better life, and Dora wasn't going to get the offer of a better job, so what were they waiting for?

'What do we do now?' he asked.

'Let's draw up the contracts,' said Coll, as though it was all a game.

'Tonight?' Dora wasn't going back on anything, but it was getting late and what was the hurry?

'I never believe in putting things off,' said Coll. 'We

must have Thea in on this. Where do we hold the conference?'

It *was* a game to him. He threw back his head as he had done before he dived into the water below the weir, before the fight at her birthday party, taking on odds but sure he could win. She was part of the stakes tonight and she would have given a great deal to deny him his triumph.

They went back to the drawing room and Coll took Simon's notebook and began to draft the agreement that his solicitors would draw up tomorrow. It sounded fine. He would do all he said, secure the lease, advance them the sum they worked out as enough to cover their debts and leave a little over for expansion.

He suggested repayment terms, and they had the bargain of a lifetime so long as Dora kept her job for six months. If she walked out then Coll could call in the debt, and she wondered if that could be what he had in mind. To make her life unbearable so that in the end she did walk out, leaving all the cards in his hands.

The light from the chandelier shone down on his smooth dark hair. He looked handsome, relaxed, happy with friends, and Simon and Thea were certainly happy; and Dora wished she could believe he had no ulterior motive.

But he wasn't acting from pure friendship. He had just admitted that and she knew he wasn't. Had Simon ever done anything to incur his enmity while they were boys? Simon had been a cheerful and popular boy, but sometimes he had been thoughtless and selfish. Children often were. He might not remember now, but it seemed more likely to Dora that Coll Sullivan had come back with a grudge, intending to harm rather than help.

'He always had to win,' Simon had said. Simon might have resented him winning sometimes and tried to belittle him, to play the boy from the Manor against the tinker's son. Coll Sullivan would remember that.

'What's wrong?' asked Thea gently, and Dora knew she was the only unrelaxed one, sitting ramrod-straight and grim-faced. Suppose she spoke up now and asked, 'Do you hate both of us? Is that what all this is about, so that you can bring us both down? Is that the secret joke?'

But he would only laugh at her. So would Simon, and she said instead, 'I feel like merchandise in a slave market, being sold to the highest bidder.'

'It's a thought,' said Coll, as though she was joking.

'Isn't it?' She met his eyes, with a challenge in her own. 'And what kind of slavemaster are you going to make?'

He went on smiling. 'You look healthy enough, you'll cope.'

'Of course she will,' said Simon breezily. 'She's famous for it—coping.'

'I think we ought to be going,' Thea suggested, and Dora was on her feet like a shot, when Coll said,

'Not you, Dora-Lily, there are still one or two things I want to discuss with you.'

Thea had realised that Dora wanted to get away, but now there was no choice. Thea and Simon had to say goodnight and leave Dora here, and Dora had to pretend she didn't care.

Kiki was collected and raised a protesting wail at being disturbed. Dora bent over the carrycot in the hall and said, 'Goodnight, sweetheart.' She kissed

Thea. 'Goodnight, see you tomorrow some time.'

Simon was still talking business with Coll, all the way to the van which stood by the steps of the front door. At the door Thea said quietly, 'Thank you. Bless you.'

Heaven bless me, thought Dora; heaven help me because I am into a situation that scares me.

'Come on, wife!' called Simon, as Thea and Dora carried the carrycot down between them.

'Wife and child,' said Thea, 'and set this down gently, I think she's waking up and wondering about supper.'

Dora stood watching them go. Her home was at the end of the drive. The warm darkness and the soft rustle of night were there too, under the same trees and the same stars. But here the night was not friendly, and when she turned Coll was standing in the doorway, and the house she had loved seemed like a waiting prison.

She could walk on, down the drive, following the white darting blur that was her small dog, and Coll couldn't stop her. He might call after her, but she didn't have to hear. Or he could follow, and she didn't want him to follow her in the darkness. She didn't want him touching her, putting a hand on her.

She went back up the steps and as she passed him, into the hall, he shut the door. Surely it hadn't sounded like that in the old days when anyone closed the front door. Tonight the hinges seemed to creak and there was a dull thud, just like you'd expect a prison door to sound.

First she had seen him as a slavemaster and now as a jailer, two roles with one thing in common. In both he was her master and her enemy.

She went back into the drawing room. 'Sit down,' he said, as he followed her.

'Thank you.' She got in a touch of sarcasm, taking the place she had just vacated. He sat down again in the chair he had been sitting in for the past half hour and said,

'Tell me what you've been doing all these years.'

She wasn't telling him anything. She hated sitting here alone with him, face to face; his eyes stripping her naked and defenceless. She countered the question. 'Don't you know all about us? You knew more about Simon's business than I did.'

He didn't answer that. Instead he said, 'I'd have expected you to be married by now.'

'I'd have thought you would.' Her face was stiff with distaste. 'If I'd thought about you at all, which I don't believe I ever did.'

He smiled at that. 'Ah yes, but I have been very busy.'

'Me too.'

'With your career?'

She worked hard, but she was still taking down someone else's dictation. She swam well and played a good fast game of tennis, and she did her own home decorating and was a very fair cook. It wasn't an impressive record of achievement set against Sullivan Properties. 'I've had better things to do with my life than money-making,' she said primly.

'So have I.' He leaned back, legs stretched and crossed at the ankles, folded arms behind his head. 'I enjoy myself. I enjoy my work and the money's very welcome, and I expect more enjoyment and more money in the future. Have you ever been married?'

He had long legs and she felt that he took up more

of the space between them than he was entitled to. She crossed her own ankles and tucked her feet back. 'No,' she said.

'Nobody good enough for you?'

Dora glared, and he laughed. 'Not still virginal?'

He was being insulting. 'Are you?' she said, and he went on laughing. He had a young face, he would probably grow old looking young, but it seemed to her that all the experience in the world was in his eyes. Then he said, feigning solicitude, 'I hope Neil Hewitt hasn't been your only lover all these years? I shouldn't like you to have missed out all along.'

Was he suggesting that Neil would be a rotten lover, and how could he know? Neil might be rampant with passion once they were alone. He wasn't, of course, he never would be, but she wasn't having Coll Sullivan sneering.

She said, 'I've missed out on nothing,' and as Coll looked disbelieving, 'I've been engaged three times and I was the one who handed the rings back, so I'm not exactly a frustrated spinster.'

'Quite the raver.' This time she deserved mocking, recounting her three failures as though they were scalps at her belt or feathers in her cap. She wasn't proud of them. She was sorry about them, and she blamed herself. A broken engagement wasn't as bad as a broken marriage, but it was still a promising relationship flawed because something was missing.

In her. She was the one who drew back because she couldn't give herself entirely and for ever. There always came a time when she could go no further in commitment and then she was alone once more, with the relief of a bird escaping from a cage.

Well, she was free again, after what must be nearly a

record in brief engagements. Neil's mother had his ring back, but Coll Sullivan was clipping her wings. 'What went wrong, three times?' he was asking, and she demanded furiously,

'What's it got to do with you? We're supposed to be discussing my job, aren't we?'

'Tonight this is your job. To sit here, in a room with me, until I say you may go.' The lightness had left his voice, it was sharp with command.

Dora remembered flouncing out of the room when he came in, and she wanted to do just that again, like the spoiled child she had been. She thought—I don't believe I can stand this, and in the silence she heard a dog bark.

'Tip,' she said, so grateful for the chance of escape that she laughed. 'He thought I was following him. I'll have to get him, I don't like him out in the dark on his own.'

'What's he likely to come up against?' Coll drawled. 'A rabbit?'

'A fox, maybe. He'd give a good account of himself, but fox bites are nasty, and he's always finding hedgehogs. They send him berserk, they roll up and they're prickly, and he finishes racing round and round them, like those old films of covered wagons and Indians, you know.'

She was at the door by now, smiling and chattering. Coll hadn't moved. 'Come back,' he said.

Her lips tightened and the smile went. 'If I don't?'

'I don't pay out.'

He meant it. If she left before he gave her permission he would tell Simon in the morning that the deal was off. Nothing was signed yet, but once the signing had been done she wouldn't put up with this treatment. She'd do a fair day's work for him, but no night duty that wasn't strictly impersonal.

She said scornfully, 'It is a touch of your white slavery, isn't it? You really do think you're buying me.' He gave her that long slow look again, that made her want to hide behind something.

'You're getting a good price for six months,' he said.

She stood feet apart, glaring at him. 'I'm getting a wage for which I'm working,' she spat. 'It's Simon's shop that needs your lousy cash, not me.'

'You need it for them,' he reminded her, and of course that was why she was here. She would have had to be starving before she would have accepted anything from him, but knowing how much it meant to Simon and Thea and Kiki was a blackmail she couldn't withstand.

She would talk to Thea tomorrow, before they got themselves tied up too tightly on legal jargon, and advise her to read the small print in any contract very carefully.

In the silence Tip yapped again and Coll said, 'I think he might have come up against that hedgehog.'

Dora closed the front door behind her, and walked slowly down the steps out of the glow of light thrown from the house. When she reached the shadows she stood, until her eyes grew accustomed to the dark, calling, 'Tip—Tip, here, boy!'

He would come in his own time, he wasn't terribly well trained, but the barking had been because he had found himself trotting home alone, not because he had tracked down a quarry. She walked through the trees that edged the drive, with the barking growing louder and closer, and when the little black and white dog came, wagging his tail, jumping up at her, she gave him a hug.

'You were quite a help just now,' she said. 'I could have been stuck in there for another hour or two if you -hadn't been out here.'

Of course she wasn't going back, and Coll could please himself what he did about it, and she hoped he would call the whole thing off. She had walked out. He had tried to give the orders and she had simply walked out, and she went on walking now, striding down the drive towards the lodge, taking deep breaths of the clean night air.

This would show him that she didn't come to heel for any man, and she went faster until she realised that she was running, heading for the lodge like a rabbit bolting for its burrow.

She stopped then and stood still, and Tip, running just ahead, stopped too and came back, and sat watching her, head on one side, small sharp ears pricked.

If she didn't go back Coll would know she was afraid of him. It wouldn't be an act of defiance, it would be admitting that she was scared. But if she could make herself go back that wouldn't be his victory, it would be hers, an exercise in discipline over herself.

He wouldn't expect her back, that should give her the advantage of surprise for a little while. She would say, 'Well, and what else do we have to discuss tonight?' Then he might agree that they had nothing, and she could leave without him guessing that she was scared.

She was sure he wouldn't be expecting her, but the front door that she had closed behind her opened when she touched it, and as she and Tip stepped into the hall Coll looked across at her from behind the reception counter. The phone was there, he might have been phoning. 'Booking in customers?' she enquired.

'We must get this out.' He touched the counter. 'Together with the rest of the hotel stuff we're not wanting. Can you check that tomorrow?'

She followed him into the drawing room. There was another log on the fire, it had been burning low, and although the night was warm Tip trotted to lie down as close as possible, nose on paws, eyes staring into the glow.

'I'll do as much as I can,' she said, 'after work.'

'Bendix and Hewitt have just dispensed with your services,' he announced.

'What did you say?' She'd heard him, she knew what he was saying. Her gasp was protest and fury because he had been on that phone just now interfering intolerably in her affairs. 'Who have you been talking to?' she gritted. 'Neil, haven't you? You've phoned Neil.'

He adjusted the log with his foot, so that sparks shot up. 'Would you believe he phoned me?'

'I would not. Why should he phone you?'

'Because he tried to ring you at the lodge, then he tried here,' he said with a maddening air of explaining everything, and it was a possible chain of events.

She demanded, 'So what did you tell him?'

'That you'd gone to get the dog in and you'd be back in a few minutes.'

So he had expected her back, unless he had said that to annoy Neil. It wouldn't have been much fun, working her month's notice out for Neil, but it would have been better than being pitchforked into Coll Sullivan's full-time service.

'And that you're starting work for me,' said Coll blandly, 'and I'd appreciate it if he'd settle for a week's notice instead of a month's. He said you weren't to worry about him, you could start with me tomorrow and he hoped you'd be very happy.'

'He didn't mean it.'

He pretended to misunderstand. 'He didn't hope you'd be happy?'

No, he probably didn't, and she certainly wouldn't. 'He didn't mean that it would be all right if I left him high and dry, without any notice,' she said shrilly. 'I shall go in in the morning and discuss with Neil how to make this break, causing the least possible inconvenience to him and his firm.'

'You've grown into a very considerate lady,' he said, with mock admiration.

'I hope I have.'

'Suppose he tries to persuade you to change your mind?'

She would have loved to say, 'I'll let him, I'd rather be working for him than you any day,' but Neil would very likely prefer another secretary in the circumstances. 'He won't,' she said.

'Or asks you to put that ring back on your finger?'

If Neil had been so anxious to talk to her tonight he might have wanted to make up the quarrel, but not after Coll had talked with him. Anyhow it wouldn't have worked. 'No,' she said.

'What was the trouble?'

He still stood by the fireplace and she walked towards a chair because she felt awkward, standing stiffly, glaring and snapping out her words. 'None of your business,' she told him for the second time.

'Jealous, is he?' he enquired affably.

It was pretty obvious from the timing of the quarrel that she might have had words with Neil about this man from her past who had kissed her on meeting.

She didn't sit down. If this was going on she wasn't staying, and Coll said, 'Coming third on your list the poor chap's bound to have qualms. If I'd known how things were I'd have shaken hands when we met again instead of kissing you.'

'You had nothing to do with it,' she lied, 'and don't bother to apologise for the kiss, because that bothered nobody, least of all me. I looked upon it as a handshake.'

'Really?' He reached her in a couple of strides, swift and silent, like something that stalks and strikes, and took her hand and in the same movement pulled her into his arms, so that her head jerked back and she had a brief glimpse of dark eyes and chiselled mouth. His mouth touched hers as her lips stretched in what might have been a scream, covering, silencing, and for a moment they were locked together in a travesty of a deep and passionate kiss.

Then he loosed her and her knees buckled, and she sat down on the chair just behind her, looking up at him with loathing. 'What the hell do you think you're doing?' she gasped thickly.

'Demonstrating the difference between a kiss and a handshake.'

'You—are—revolting!' She had to gulp in breath between each word, she felt as though she had been running for miles.

'You haven't changed much either,' he said. Dora was sure her hair was standing on end, but he didn't have a hair out of place. He was cool as a cucumber, and so calm that her blazing outrage was dampened down.

She had claimed sexual experience. He had no right to touch her, much less kiss her in that fashion, but she could hardly react now like a threatened virgin. She would not for the world have had him suspect that was what she was. She would be as blasé as he, and she said coldly, 'I thought you said this was to be a hands-off arrangement.'

'So I did.' He sounded as though she was reminding him of some small unimportant clause. 'Would it bother you if I tried to seduce you?'

He was needling her, trying to shock and harass her, and she made a small grimace. 'You couldn't bother me, you might bore me.'

That wasn't true. He could have her on a rack of tension. He stood looking down at her, and from somewhere she remembered his breath on her cheek, in a forgotten moment of closeness. She really did detest him. The conceit of it, suggesting that she couldn't resist him!

'Seduction's no risk,' she said scornfully, 'but I'd like your assurance that you don't go in for rape.'

'You have it.' He chuckled, 'Perhaps we should have that written into the contract. How shall we word it?'

'Do you mind?' She got up, throwing it all off as a poor joke. 'I've had enough. Can I go home now?'

'You wouldn't like your old room?'

'In your house? Not likely!'

'Shall I walk you home?' he offered.

'Why?'

'Protection?'

'Who'd protect me against you?' she enquired cuttingly, and he laughed.

'Goodnight, Dora-Lily.'

'Don't——' She was going to say, 'Don't call me that,' but it was too trivial to make an issue of. She had more to worry about than him tacking Lilias on to Dora. 'Don't bother to see me out,' she said. 'Goodnight. Come on, Tip,' and she walked out again into the night, and once more made her way towards the comparative safety of her own small home.

She would talk to Thea tomorrow, she'd tell her about the pearls and about tonight. Thea would be concerned about the pearls. It didn't say much for his character that Coll Sullivan had been a thief, but she would be more amused than shocked to hear that he had just made a pass at Dora.

She thought that Dora was able to look after herself in most man–woman situations, and Dora was, of course. You could be a virgin and still know your way around. It didn't mean you were naïve. It was more likely to mean that you kept a cool head and your wits about you.

Dora wasn't going to lose her head over a man she heartily disliked, but she was realising now that she had challenged him with her antagonism.

'There's no danger of you seducing me,' she had said, so he would almost certainly try. Coll always had to win, and if anything could make her run it would be him, circling her, closing in, marking her down as prey.

CHAPTER FIVE

At first sight of Neil next morning Dora choked up. She didn't know whether she ought to be starting with an apology or an explanation. But she felt she was in the wrong, and Neil wasn't going to help.

She was at her small desk in his office, with the morning mail around her. He was a few minutes late and he had stomped through the outer office, grunting at the good mornings he'd received, flung open his door, and stood transfixed when he spotted Dora.

Then he demanded accusingly, 'What are you doing here?' as though she was a burglar.

Jenny the filing clerk, nearest the door, gasped. She knew there was only Dora in there, and Dora was Mr Hewitt's secretary and fiancée, and why shouldn't she be in his office?

As he shut the door behind him Jenny asked the rest of the outer office, there were three of them, 'What's biting him?'

'Didn't you expect me?' said Dora.

'Not after last night.' Neil hung up his lightweight mac carefully on a hanger on the hatstand, and placed his briefcase squarely on his desk. Then he sat down, looking severe and dignified, and after a few seconds Dora asked him,

'What did Coll say?'

'That you were going to work for him,' said Neil huffily.

'Yes, I suppose I am.' She had opened about half the post. She had one letter half out of the envelope. She took it out and wondered whether she should read it or whether Neil would prefer her to drop everything and leave immediately.

He was glowering at her, and she said, 'That's what we were discussing last night—work.' Then she remembered Coll kissing her savagely and brutally, and her face flamed as guiltily as though it had been her doing.

Neil would have had to be blind not to suspect that she was hiding something, but if she told him everything it wouldn't help. He would interpret it his way, and he had misjudged her every action since Coll Sullivan returned.

If she said, 'I can't stand the man, but he kissed me last night and warned me he'll try to make love to me,' Neil would assume she had flirted with Coll. 'So why are you going to work for him?' he'd ask her, and he wouldn't accept anything as good enough reason.

She said, 'He's investing in the antique shop and we're going to get the house how he wants it, and I'm going to do some secretarial work.'

He eyed her burning face and said nothing, and Dora began to read the letter she had just opened because she could look down at it and avoid his gaze.

One of Neil's clients thought he had been overcharged in income tax and was explaining at length why. 'Why are you here?' Neil demanded abruptly, and she asked,

'Don't you want me to stay until you find a replacement?'

He didn't realise how much she did, nor how awkward it would be for him if he didn't let her hand over to her successor, explaining all sorts of things.

'I'd rather get a temp in,' he said vehemently, as though he would prefer anyone, untrained, unco-

operative, anything, rather than her, and she said,
'I understand.'

'Mother expected this all along.'

Dora put the opened mail on top of the unopened
and began to take small personal belongings out of her
drawers and drop them into her handbag. She didn't
have much here, but she couldn't come back for it.
Neil sounded as though he would put everything she
left behind into the dustbins the moment she walked
out of the door.

'Mother said I'm lucky you haven't treated me like
you did Peter Marsden,' he said bitterly, and Dora
curled up inside. Mrs Hewitt *would* say that! She
never wanted Neil to marry, but getting the ring back
within days would be a blow to any mother's pride in
her son.

'Your mother's right,' she said. 'You deserve someone
nicer than me.'

She went out of the office wearing her coat loose over
her shoulders, carrying her bulging handbag, and
Jenny chased her into the pavement to ask, 'What's the
matter?'

'I've got another job,' said Dora.

'You *haven't*?' Jenny looked for Dora's ring and
squealed, 'You're not wearing your ring! I *say*, is it all
off?'

'Yes.'

Jenny trotted beside her into the yard where the
cars were parked. She would have loved to ask lots of
questions but Dora was walking fast and didn't seem
in a mood for talking. When she got into her Mini she
gave Jenny a wan smile.

'See you, Jen,' she said.

She drove carefully because she was feeling shaky.

She was sure that Neil would be happier with another secretary since the engagement had ended, but the parting should have been less acrimonious. Coll had done that last night. If Dora had handed in her notice herself she would have made it less abrupt, and tried to explain and apologise.

She wondered again who had phoned who. She had meant to ask Neil if Coll had called him the moment her back was turned, or if it *had* been Neil seeking her out. She also wondered what Coll had said to Neil when they were alone in the Manor on Sunday evening, with Simon and Thea going through the upstairs rooms, and Dora standing by her old bedroom window watching night fall.

'I can't imagine what they're finding to talk about,' she had said to Thea, but Thea's. 'Can't you?' had sounded as though Thea had ideas on the subject.

Dora, maybe! They could have been discussing her. Beforehand Neil had been suspicious and touchy, but afterwards he had been riven with jealousy, furiously demanding impossible promises.

How *dare* he? Coll, not Neil. Neil was not a daring man, he had probably never taken a real chance in his life. Except in asking Dora to marry him, because with her record she had to be a risk.

Her first engagement had been too soon, she had been too young, barely eighteen. At that time everyone was sorry for her, her father's death was fresh in their minds and the changed fortunes of the Holcrofts was still a shock. Patrick was a prosperous farmer's son, and he could have offered her a life not all that different from the one she had been born to.

There were horses in the stables behind the farm-house and he couldn't see why Dora was taking a shorthand-typing course when she would have been happier riding and enjoying herself. And he couldn't see why she wouldn't marry him right away, and then she would have had their home to occupy herself with because she couldn't like living in the old lodge with old Granny Drayton.

When she got through her course she took her first job, and was almost relieved that Patrick made a fuss about it because by then she knew that she didn't want to marry him.

There was a fuss, but it died down and two years later Patrick married another girl, and the only reason Dora and Simon were no longer close friends with Patrick's family and friends was that they couldn't afford to be. They were in a different income bracket, but Dora had never regretted parting from Patrick.

The second engagement was the one she felt worst about, because she was older by then and she should have known better, but Peter Marsden was the most importunate in her circle of admirers. She always had admirers, she was an attractive-looking girl with a lively personality that drew friends and would-be lovers to her.

Peter Marsden managed a largish electrical shop in town and he and Dora were supposed to be getting married at Easter. It was all arranged, that was the dreadful part. The wedding reception, the honeymoon, everything had been arranged. She had her wedding dress, and Thea was to be matron of honour, and then she knew she couldn't go through with it.

All along she had tried to slow things down, but there was the flat over the shop where Peter worked and she thought she loved him, until the panic began to build up.

'What's wrong with me?' she asked herself a hundred times. 'I do love him. My heart melts when he touches me, and I like him, and there's no one I'd rather spend the rest of my life with, but I can't marry him.'

She ran to Thea, just a week before she should have been married, and started babbling incoherently, 'What am I going to do? Everybody says it's pre-wedding nerves, but it isn't, I can't *marry* him. What am I going to *do?*'

Up till then Thea had suggested it was pre-wedding nerves too, but then she had said, 'We'd better start sending back the wedding presents.'

There had been much more fuss that time, and Dora could understand why Neil and his mother were congratulating themselves they hadn't featured in a repetition of that. It was plain that she wasn't meant to marry. She was allergic to marriage, although with Thea and Simon as her closest examples she should have been all for it.

Maybe it was because she had once thought that her father was strong and that her life was safe, and then overnight there had been nothing left. Perhaps that made her unable to trust one man entirely again.

Whatever the reason she wasn't making a great success of her personal life, and all the immediate future offered seemed to be trouble and a chance of destruction.

Now there she *was* being melodramatic! She tried to smile at herself as she parked the car behind the shop, and went in through the back door into Simon's workshop. Coll Sullivan couldn't destroy them. He could make things very unpleasant and he would, for her at any rate, but he couldn't destroy her and she wondered why she was finding it impossible to smile.

Simon wasn't in the workshop. Dora went into the empty shop and called up the stairs, 'Anybody home and Thea appeared within seconds, carrying Kiki, and with Tip underfoot.

Dora dropped Tip in each morning before she left for work. She opened the back door and in he trotted. Sometimes she looked in if she had a few minutes to spare, but this morning she hadn't felt like talking until she'd seen Neil.

'You're back early,' said Thea. From the top of the stairs she gave the shop a quick glance around, although she would have heard customers enter by the ringing of the front doorbell, Tip always yapped to alert her. 'Come on up.'

She was rushing through her morning chores, and she led the way back into the kitchen, replacing Kiki in a playpen, then darting into the bedroom to finish making the bed. 'Why are you back early?' she called.

Dora peered into an empty coffee pot and filled the kettle. 'Because I'm not working my month's notice for Neil. Coll spoke to him on the phone last night and said I was working for him, and this morning Neil heaved me out.'

'Oh,' said Thea.

'Where's Simon?' Dora switched on the kettle, and came to stand in the doorway of the bedroom. Kiki was beating a drum with a wooden building brick and the sound was echoing in Dora's head.

'Gone to London with Coll,' said Thea. She pushed the duvet into shape and looked up a little anxiously. 'They're seeing the lawyers. You wouldn't have wanted to go on working for Neil, would you?'

Everything was rushing on and Dora had no say in

any of it. Neither had Thea and Simon. Who could say 'No' to an offer like Coll Sullivan's? She said fervently, 'I only hope and pray that Simon reads every line of anything he signs, particularly the small print,' and at that Thea straightened, smiling, trying to be reassuring.

'But of course he will, you're not the only one with brains in the family.'

It was nothing to do with brains. Simon had been a first-class student, getting excellent grades. He was a very intelligent man, but, 'He trusts Coll and I don't,' Dora said bluntly.

'Why don't you?'

The two girls faced each other and Dora said heavily, 'He's a thief for one thing—I do know that.'

'You mean he used to be? When he was a boy, travelling with his father who got his living in scrap metal and clapped-out old cars?'

Thea always looked for the best in everyone, and now she was going to remind Dora that the moral standard of the two children at the Manor House might not apply to the tinker's son. In him light fingers might be less of a crime.

'Very likely,' said Dora, 'but if he took anything in the early days I never heard about it. I'm talking about the last time he came while we were living in the Manor. He was twenty then and he took my pearls.'

'Your *pearls*?' That was before Thea came into Dora's life, and she looked shocked.

'They weren't worth all that much.' Dora went back to Kiki and tried to take the drum away. Kiki resisted, she didn't want to bang a woolly rabbit, she wanted to bang a drum, and faced with a tantrum or another tattoo Dora put the drum down again, and sat down to wait for the kettle to boil.

'How much?' asked Thea.

'I don't know. They were real, but it was a small necklace that had belonged to my mother. It was the only thing I had of my mother's, my father gave it to me on my sixteenth birthday. It was about six months later that Coll came.' Her face was pale and set. 'We hadn't seen him for years and he just turned up one evening, about the same time of year, the summer like he always used to.' She spoke jerkily, as though she was intent on keeping the account brief and telling nothing but the bare facts.

'Simon was home from Oxford and we were in the drawing room and I was going out somewhere and putting my pearls on. It was a party or something, Simon was supposed to have been going too. The clasp was awkward, so I didn't wear the pearls. I left them on a table and—he took them.'

Thea frowned, shrugged, gestured bewilderment. 'What do you mean, took them? Did he just put them in his pocket? Didn't you ask for them back? What did Simon say about it? And your father?'

'My father wasn't there, I think he'd gone to a race meeting somewhere.' Dora managed a faint grin. 'Simon was livid when I said Coll had taken them. He said I'd worn them and lost them, the fastener was faulty, they had slipped off before, and I was a bit careless in those days.'

'But you don't think that happened?'

'No.'

The kettle boiled and Thea made the coffee. Kiki went on banging the drum, accompanying it with a chant given at full lung power, and Dora rubbed the

spot between her eyebrows where the frown was set-
tling.

'Hush, darling,' said Thea, scooping up the drum.
'We can't hear the customers.' Kiki roared with fury,
and as suddenly accepted the situation and the rusk
that Thea offered her.

Dora was remembering it all again. She hadn't gone
to that party after all, she had gone riding instead.
Simon wasn't going now that Coll had turned up, so
why should she? She had been out of the house for
about two hours and when she came back Coll and
Simon were listening to the hi-fi. She had gone up to
her own room, and woken early and come downstairs
for a glass of milk.

That was when she had found that her pearls were
missing, and she had gone to Simon's room to ask if
he'd seen them.

He was in bed, still asleep, when she started to
question him, leaning over him and shaking his shoulder. 'No,' he'd said, and buried his head in the pillow.

'I left them on a table in the drawing room. Nobody's been in there, have they?'

'At this time in the morning?' It wasn't seven o'clock
yet, the house was silent and his voice was muffled by
the pillow.

'Well, they've gone.' The staff had all been with the
family for years, and the pearls had been lying around
in her bedroom for months. They had gone when Coll
had come.

'What's gone?' Simon had mumbled.

'My mother's pearls.' Her voice had risen shrilly.
'Where's Coll?'

And then Simon had yawned and stretched and sat
up asking, 'Why?'

'Where is he? Is he here? Is he coming back?'

'No.' She had been sure then. She remembered now how she had felt then.

'He's staying at the Fleece,' Simon had said. 'I asked him to stay here, but he said he'd booked in there for the night.'

'I'll bet he's booked out now,' she had said fiercely, and rushed out of the room. Simon, grabbing a robe, had followed her shouting,

'Where are you going?'

'To think, aren't I?'

She had run down the stairs and out of the house, and gone on running all the way down the drive and along the road until she came to the green and the village pub.

She had gone to the back door where the landlord had answered her knock, surprised to see her, saying, 'Miss Holcroft?' as though he wasn't sure he recognised her although he knew her.

'Do you have a man called Sullivan staying here?' she had asked.

'Yes.'

'Could I speak to him, please?'

'He's having breakfast. Go on up.'

She had gone to the dining room which ran the full length of the eaves; black beams and white stuccoed walls, and a dozen or so tables, with red lamps and red napkins on white tablecloths, laid for tonight.

The Fleece was famous for ham and egg suppers, but there was only one overnight room, and Coll sat at the far end, at a table laid for breakfast. He was eating toast, she remembered, and drinking coffee, and wearing jeans and a faded blue shirt.

When he saw her his eyes narrowed, and she waited

until she was right by his table before she spoke.
'You're leaving early, aren't you?' she said.

'So?'

'I'm lucky to catch you.'

'You think so?'

She held the back of the chair that faced him, so
tightly that her fingers hurt, somehow that seemed to
steady her voice when she said, 'You wouldn't have
picked up my pearls last night, would you? Absent-
mindedly?'

He started to grin. 'Lost them, have you?'

'I know where I left them.'

'But you don't know where they are now?'

'I think I might.'

'Prove it.' The grin was triumphant, and she knew
that she could prove nothing, they wouldn't be found
on him.

What had he done with them? Hidden them?
Posted them? She could accuse him, call in the local
policeman and prove nothing, and Simon would be
furious with her and so would her father.

But Coll Sullivan had taken her mother's pearls,
and he said now, with a savage bitterness, 'You self-
satisfied little slag, it's time somebody took something
away from you.'

No one had ever spoken to her like that before, no
one had robbed her before. She wanted to hit him,
claw him, but she knew that if she tried he would hit
her, and she hunted wildly for words to throw at him
like stones, to bruise him with. All she could find was,
'You—you gipsy-scum!'

That didn't hurt him. He didn't flinch at that. He
said, 'Not gipsy-scum, tinker-scum.'

'All right then, keep them,' she flared. 'Much good will they do you!'

'Thank you.' He sounded as though she really was giving him a gift, and she hissed at him,

'Where is your father? In jail?'

He still didn't flinch, although she knew now that that must have hurt. 'Thank you for everything,' he said, and she turned and he called after her, 'Don't worry, this time I won't be back...'

There was a cup of coffee in front of her on the kitchen table, and Thea was coming in, from serving a customer down in the shop.

'So you think he just took off with the pearls?' said Thea.

'Yes.'

'But Simon thought you'd lost them?'

'Yes.'

'Could you have lost them?'

'It's possible,' she conceded, but she was convinced that Coll had taken them, although she could never prove it. She could only warn Thea so that, however Simon felt, Thea would be a little on her guard.

'It's water under the bridge, isn't it?' Thea sighed. All this had happened ten years ago and today was what counted, but Dora suspected that Coll Sullivan was still taking from the Holcrofts, not giving.

She said, 'After you'd gone last night he asked if I'd mind if he tried to seduce me,' and Thea's face cleared, the worried look dissolving into laughter.

'Did he? He was giving you fair warning, wasn't he?'

'I would mind,' said Dora.

'Of course you would.' But Thea was still laughing. 'But it's an ordinary healthy lusty male attitude. Most men must fancy a knock-out of a girl like you.'

'Why, thank you,' said Dora, smiling too, although it wasn't like that at all. Coll Sullivan didn't admire her, he despised her, he would humiliate her if he could.

It wasn't going to happen, but even talking about him making love to her made her head ache and her throat close up so that it was hard to swallow her coffee.

She picked up her handbag and started to empty it on to the kitchen table: an assortment of pens, four lipsticks, a pocket calculator, a pair of tights in a cellophane pack, a red and white spotted headscarf, two nail varnishes, a bottle of moisturiser, a jar of cleansing pads and a large packet of safety pins.

'Not much to show for two years, is it?' she said. 'And another broken engagement.'

'And that,' said Thea, pointing to her daughter, who was clutching the bars of the baby-pen and trying to shake them loose.

'Thanks to you and Simon,' said Dora.

'She's part yours, though, isn't she?'

'Oh yes, please!'

'And I've got a feeling that the next two years are going to be a lot better,' said Thea, looking wise and knowing, trying to cheer Dora up.

'It's the next six months that are making me break out in a cold sweat,' said Dora wryly. 'Here,' she pushed the lipsticks into a little pile, 'have a lipstick.'

Thea tried them all out on her wrist, scoring four lines in varying reds and presenting a gory spectacle. 'I'll have these two,' she decided.

Dora swept the rest of her office souvenirs back into her handbag. 'Well,' she said, 'I'm working for Coll

Sullivan now. I've got to make a list of furniture up there that won't be needed—well, that I think won't be needed. You and Simon made some notes, didn't you?'

'I'll get them.' Thea brought the notebook from the bureau in the living room, and asked anxiously, 'You will be all right?'

'On my own, you mean?' Thea nodded. 'I've got to get used to it, and you can't shut up the shop.'

Dora didn't want to go up to the Manor alone, but there were a lot of things she didn't want to be doing that she would have to do in the next six months.

'I'll close early,' Thea offered. 'I'll come up about four.'

'Oh, please.' By four o'clock this afternoon Thea would be very a welcome sight. 'Where's the key?'

It was in a drawer, in the kitchen, and Thea handed it over. It was heavy, a heavy old dark key to the back door of the Manor house, and Dora held it, weighing it in her hand, remembering the shape of it. It had always been in the lock in the old days. She had never held it before.

The key to her past and her future. 'They made them to last, didn't they?' she commented. There were keys like this downstairs in the shop. People bought them for ornaments. Keys to old houses that had gone.

'See you later,' she said. 'Come on, Tip. If I need company I can always talk to you.'

She drove past the lodge. That seemed strange, she had never done that before in her little car, always turned and tucked it comfortably in beside the lodge. But this morning she drove up the drive, and round to the garages that had been part of the stable block. She got out of the car, leaving it in the open, and turned the key in the lock of the back door and stepped into the house that had been her home. ·

She went straight through into the hall, because it was obvious what had to go from here. The counter, the shelves behind, the rack where newspapers had been displayed.

Simon had suggestions in his little book, and she wished he hadn't put down a grandfather clock and an oak settle. Because those things had been here before. It wouldn't be the same clock, nor the same settle, but she would have preferred as little as possible to remind her of the house she had grown up in.

She went from room to room, as Thea and Simon had done. They had jotted down suggestions of furniture Coll might want them to look for, in some cases pieces Simon knew he could get. Dora was doing the take-away job, suggesting what might go.

Some was obvious. Some she was less sure about because she didn't know what Coll Sullivan's tastes were. He'd said he wanted the house back as near as possible in period, and he had the money to do it. But pictures, for instance. There was nothing valuable, but there were pretty prints in the bedrooms and some quite attractive landscapes in the downstairs rooms. Some of them she liked, but she didn't know what kind of pictures he'd want on his walls.

It was very quiet. She could hear birds singing outside, but in here, except for the occasional creak of old timbers, there was only the sound of her own footsteps and breathing; and Tip keeping close because this was a big empty house and he didn't fancy being lost in it.

She wished she had brought a radio along. The TV had gone from the drawing room, and there was nothing to switch on to fill the silence. As a rule she didn't mind silence. She was alone most of the time in her little home, and she took silence for granted. It didn't make her lonely the way this silence did.

The trouble was that she was listening for voices she was never going to hear. She would get used to it. After a while there would be other voices and the house would have moved with the times, but tomorrow, if she was up here tomorrow, she would bring a radio.

When the phone bell rang it seemed to shatter the air. It wasn't very loud. It rang in the hall, on the reception desk, and Dora was in one of the rooms leading off the hall. But she nearly dropped a tin box she had just picked up, the ringing seemed so loud in the silence.

She thought it might be Thea, or Simon. She didn't want to think it might be Coll, but when she gave the number he said, 'Dora-Lily?'

'No,' she said tartly, 'it's the Grey Lady. Didn't you know the place is haunted?'

He chuckled. 'Is that a fact?'

'At the moment, no,' she said, 'but in future very likely.'

'By you? You'd never make a Grey Lady.'

'After I've worked for you for six months my hair could be snow-white, let alone grey.'

'You are working for me? Neil told you to run along?'

He knew what Neil would tell her. He had seen to it that she got no support from Neil. 'More or less,' she said. 'He also told me you phoned him last night.'

'Then he's a liar,' said Coll cheerfully.

She would probably never know who phoned whom, but as she hadn't asked Neil she couldn't argue. She asked, 'Has Simon signed everything you put in front of him?'

'Oh yes.'

'Well, I haven't.'

'You don't need to, do you?' he drawled. 'In this case one Holcroft signature is as good as two.'

He was right. Simon had signed for Thea and Kiki, and Dora was hostage for them all. She made her voice brisk, businesslike and impersonal. 'What's happening about this furniture? The stuff that's here now?'

'We keep what we want. The rest goes to auction.' He meant what he wanted, of course, although he was pretending he valued their advice.

'You haven't bought the job lot?'

'No. I buy what I want. The rest stays Mrs Wardour's property and that's how she's disposing of it. I'm getting it cleared and carted because I need it out of the way.'

That meant the clearing would be fast and efficient. He would give orders and the wagons would roll. 'Well, I'm making this list of what I think you won't need,' she said, 'but I don't know what you want.'

'Don't you?' She could see him, against the misty background of an office somewhere. She could see his smile when he said, 'I thought we both understood that last night,' and as she slammed down the phone she heard him say, 'See you this evening.'

Last night he had said he wanted her, and it would be a long time before she could forget that violating kiss. But she wished that she had pretended to misunderstand him now and acted as though he was still talking about the furniture.

She had flung the phone away as though it was his hand pushing back her hair, touching her cheek. She had betrayed how jittery she was, but next time she would be thick-skinned as a rhino, impervious to the most obvious innuendo.

For crying out loud, she wasn't sixteen any longer. She was twenty-six, and she could have had a dozen lovers. Some of the lovers she could have had had been very pushy men, but she had never slammed down a phone before, quivering with outrage.

Thea had suggested that Coll Sullivan was an ordinary healthy lusty male. Like most women Dora could handle them, and found them both endearing and amusing. But he was not endearing, nor amusing, nor ordinary; and he wouldn't see her this evening. She would have finished work for the day and cleared off, long before he got back.

She went home to the lodge to type out her lists, sitting by the window so that she saw Thea walk by, pushing the pram. She leaned out of the window and called 'Hi, the pair of you,' then she opened the front door and helped Thea lift the pram in.

They released Kiki and gave her a pile of toys to play with on the hearthrug, and Dora went back to her typing table and picked up several pages and said, 'Have a look at this. Left-hand column's what I think he might want to keep, right-hand's what I suggest getting rid of.'

Instead of taking the papers from her Thea asked, 'Have you had any lunch?'

'I had a cup of tea when I got back.'

Thea did what Simon called her 'mother hen shudder'—clucking disapprovingly with ruffled feathers. 'Honestly, Dora, you are an *idiot*! You can't go all day without food, especially a day like this which has been upsetting all along.'

She went into the kitchen, opening a cupboard for a tin of soup. 'We don't want you flaking out in Coll Sullivan's arms,' she said.

Dora felt the grip of his arms around her and stiffened, holding the sheets of paper tighter. 'We do not,' she agreed. 'But didn't you say he was just a nice ordinary man, not the sort to take advantage?'

'I never did.' Thea sounded emphatic. 'Mushroom or tomato?'

'Either.' Neither really, she wasn't hungry, but Thea was going to heat up one or the other and watch that Dora drank it.

'There's something dangerous about him,' said Thea very quietly, 'but——'

'But we need the money,' Dora finished. 'So I'll drink my soup and then I won't faint from hunger in his arms. Anyhow, I'm going out to dinner tonight. He phoned and said he'd see me later but I won't be here.'

'Who are you having dinner with?' The only man Dora had been dating for months was Neil, and she smiled at Thea's surprise.

'Nothing exciting. A very small hen party.'

It could hardly have been a smaller party, because she ate alone, sitting on a high stool at a snack bar in a town eight miles away. Then she went to a cinema alone—a thing she could never remember doing before—all to keep out of the way of Coll Sullivan tonight.

She had left her lists on the counter in the hall of the Manor House, and a note that she would be available from nine o'clock in the morning if he would care to leave instructions.

Thea knew Dora was dodging Coll, and Thea hadn't asked again where Dora was going, nor who the girls were. If Coll questioned Thea she wouldn't be able to tell him a thing. But she didn't realise that Dora was going out on her own.

There were plenty of homes Dora could have visited, or she could have phoned around and got herself a companion at short notice. But whoever she saw she would have to talk about the new master of the Manor, and how she and Simon had been put on his payroll, and that was not a subject on which she wished to close her day.

The film wasn't up to much, but it served its purpose. It passed the time. She got home around eleven o'clock, and she was in the bathroom with the bathwater running when the phone rang.

There were friends who might be calling her this late, but she wondered how long it would be before she could hear a phone ring near her without a flare of panic and a reluctance to pick up the receiver.

She had to answer. It might be someone else, it might be that he would ring through the night until she answered, but when he spoke it took all her resolution not to put down the receiver again.

She said, 'Do you know what time it is?'

'Of course. I have to see you.'

'Now? Not a chance. I'll be along in the morning.'

'Now. Here. I did tell you I expected to see you this evening.'

'I had a date,' she explained.

'You're home now. I'll give you ten minutes then I'll walk down to the lodge and fetch you.'

He would. He would bang on the door. He had no consideration for anyone. He had spoken curtly until then, but suddenly he laughed. 'Don't be scared, I'm not going to leap on you.'

'I'm not scared.' She couldn't have him coming here and marching her off, and she would feel a fool locking her door against him. She said with as much hauteur as she could summon, 'I'll be along, and you'd better make what you've got to say brief and to the point, because when I get there I'll give you ten minutes.'

Her head buzzed like a hive of angry bees, and she could have screamed at him for being a tinpot dictator. 'When I whistle you'll come,' he'd said. What else could she do this time? But when she got there she'd have something to say about his attitude.

She dashed back to turn off the tap, and pulled her dress over her head again, then got into shoes and buttoned up her coat.

She walked fast, hoping that the breeze would cool her hot cheeks, looking for all the world like a girl hurrying through the night to meet a lover.

CHAPTER SIX

DORA heard footsteps on the rough gravel of the drive briefly before she saw him, a tall dark figure coming for her like a ghost. Who said the Manor wasn't haunted? A lot of people had lived and died here, but most of them had been her ancestors, and this shadow was no kin. He was the enemy.

She walked in the centre of the drive and so did he. She would walk straight into him if they both kept on their present path, straight into his arms, a head-on collision. So let him move aside or stop, she was hanged if she'd start hopping about.

But of course there wasn't a collision. Of course he stopped and so did she, when they were face to face and about a foot apart. Dora had walked so fast that her breath was catching, or perhaps it was having him so close. 'You'd better have a good reason for this,' she said.

'Had a good evening?'

'Hilarious.'

He grinned at her. 'Then it wasn't Neil.'

She ignored that, but it was fair reasoning, she had never done much laughing with Neil. She wasn't here to chat and she walked beside him without saying another word, expecting him to break the silence. But he didn't, all the way up to the house and round, past the garages, to the far end of the stable block.

Coll opened the top half of the door and she heard a faint whinny and the sound of a horse getting to its feet, and then a chestnut head was thrust out. The neck was arched and strong, the head tapered to a very small muzzle and Dora gasped, 'Oh, you're beautiful! What's your name? Where did you come from?'

'Damozel,' said Coll. 'I had them stabled in London.'

'Them?' But she only had eyes for this one, she was still talking to it when he said,

'Coming riding?'

He was leading another horse, a big black hunter, and it was a challenge she couldn't refuse. Not that she wanted to refuse. 'Yes, please,' she said.

'Here,' he offered her his reins, and went to open the stable door and saddle and bridle the little Arab.

Dora felt as excited as a child offered a surprise treat. This was taking sweets from a stranger, but she could hardly wait for him to slip the final buckle.

The mare stood quietly while she mounted and then Coll swung into his saddle and the hooves clattered over the flagstones as the two horses trotted side by side out of the courtyard.

The last time Dora had ridden over these stones she had been very young. The horses had been sold when the house was sold, and she had cried herself sick because they were living and loved. Her horse and Simon's and her father's. It hadn't been the same riding from the farm when she was engaged to Patrick, and that had been a long time ago too.

She would have been happy to let the horse go where it wanted. There was a paddock behind the house, she would have been happy cantering around that for a while, but Coll was a little ahead, so little that it could have been a photo-finish in a race, but the hunter took the lead and the mare followed.

Coll didn't speak, and she was glad. She was very conscious of him, of course, and if she couldn't be alone she wished almost anyone else was riding with her. But they went quietly the whole length of the village, without passing a soul.

There were still lights on in the Fleece, but the customers had all gone home. Upstairs they would be laying tables for tomorrow. There might be someone staying in the one bedroom who would have breakfast up there in the morning, and very much against her will Dora found herself looking up.

Coll must know what she was remembering. The last thing she wanted to do was turn her head just then and meet his eyes, but she couldn't help it and she knew he would be smiling.

'We must continue that conversation some time,' he said.

'I'd be fascinated.'

They were almost out of the village now, and he dug his heels into his horse's flanks, moving off towards the open country; and Dora went too, the little mare galloping smoothly and swiftly at a touch.

It was as exhilarating as a break for freedom. Coll galloped beside her and she knew that his horse could outrace hers, but with the wind rushing through her hair she felt as though she was riding Pegasus, winged leaving the world behind.

The hooves thundered on the turf, and she heard herself laughing, and the only hitch was that the couldn't gallop all night, only where the ground was level and firm and there was no risk of the horses stumbling.

She reined and the black hunter checked pace, and Coll waited and they went on together, side by side, sometimes close, sometimes drawing apart, aiming for nowhere in particular, just riding under the night stars.

They said nothing to each other, for half an hour perhaps more, and then the horses brushed and she could have touched him and she laughed again. 'I'd forgotten,' she said. 'I had.'

'Not how to ride,' he said.

'How marvellous it is. Where did you ride?'

'Richmond Park, mostly.'

She wondered who usually sat in this saddle and how long it would be before she came to stake her claim. It would be a 'she', and the sooner she came the better. With a girl-friend around to occupy Coll's spare time Dora's six-month stint might not be so bad after all.

This ride had blown a lot of cobwebs away. She was feeling wonderfully alive and awake, although it must be after midnight, and an hour ago she had been ready to crawl into a hot bath and then fall into bed.

'Must we go back?' she said, not meaning that, just meaning—this has been wonderful.

'No,' said Coll.

Oh, but yes, they must. She would have loved to gallop away from her worries, but he would have galloped beside her. She wondered if he might ever let her ride Loki, the hunter, and wondered at herself for thinking of asking a favour.

They came back quietly so that the horses were cool when they reached the stables. As she dismounted Dora asked, 'Who's looking after them?'

'There'll be a groom along in the morning.'

'I could have done it.'

Coll made no answer to that. He led the hunter into the next stable, switching on lights, and Dora took off the tack and rubbed Damozel down. There was straw underfoot, and the old familiar smells, and it was so like the old times that she almost believed it would be Simon out there, or the groom of her father's day.

She wasn't sure about Coll's motives tonight. He might simply have wanted her to know there were horses in the stables again—after all, she was coming up in the morning to take over. It was the sort of thing that had to be mentioned. He had summoned her and she had had to come, that might have amused him.

If he was out to dissolve her antagonism—he had warned her he would try to seduce her—it had been a possible ploy. Exciting, different. Come ride with me by moonlight. He on the stronger faster horse, she following his lead.

The horses were his, the stables belonged to him, and the house. She hoped he didn't presume that today's contract with Simon made her one of his possessions.

She didn't want to walk out to him now. But he was waiting when she came out and closed the stable door behind her. 'Bedded down?' he asked.

'Yes. Thank you. I enjoyed myself. What do I do tomorrow?'

He took a couple of steps that brought him close to her. 'I've written it out for you.'

It was dark so you would step closer to anyone you were talking to, it didn't mean this was going to be more than talk, but instinctively she moved away, turning swiftly so that her hair swished across his face.

Perhaps he put a hand to brush it away and his fingers caught in the tangles. Or perhaps he did grab her by the hair, because he held her forcing her face round, and she gasped, 'What has Simon signed?'

'He'll tell you tomorrow.'

If she tugged it would hurt. If she stood still he would have to loose her. 'A contract between friends?' she asked through gritted teeth.

'Of course.'

'That's what Simon thinks.'

He was still holding her hair, she could feel his fingers in the long tresses, and she kept her head very still, looking steadily into his eyes. She said, 'Do you know you're the only enemy I've ever had?'

'Am I now?'

Any animosity she had encountered until now, even

Mrs Hewitt's, had been petty. There had been no one who threatened her as this man did, not even the quiet official men who took away everything after her father died. She asked, 'Do you have many enemies?'

'Oh yes,' he said softly, 'but you are special.'

'So are you.'

Suddenly he laughed, letting her hair slide between his fingers, and she clapped both hands to her head, pushing her hair back and holding it down, as though a loose tendril would put her at risk of being grabbed again. 'You should cherish your enemies,' he said, 'they sharpen the senses.'

She snapped, 'I'm learning that,' and he laughed again.

'It won't be all I'll teach you before we're through.'

'Oh, get lost!' That sounded pert and puerile, but she was losing her cool, and he drawled,

'I'm home, you're the one who might get lost.'

'Not tonight,' she said, and went striding away.

She always seemed to be rushing these days, either running to the lodge or running to the Manor House. She had come out in such a tearing hurry and temper that Tip hadn't managed to slip out with her, and he was waiting for her now.

'It was as well you didn't make it,' she told him. 'I don't know what I'd have done with you while I was galloping all over the heath.'

That ride had been the most thrilling thing that had happened to her in ages. She began to smile at the bliss of it, taking off her coat and shoes, going into the bathroom and getting out of her clothes. The bath-water was tepid, but it was too late to bother empty-ing and running more hot water, so she splashed her-self down, washing quickly and towelling briskly.

Her hair was like a gorse bush when she tried to pull a comb through it, and she put down the comb and picked up a brush, looking at her reflection in the bathroom mirror as she tried to tame her hair. She was wearing a short shift-shirt in white cotton and her shiny clean face was not the most glamorous sight.

A sudden tug, as the brush hooked a tangle, reminded her of Coll, of the way her hair had blown across his face, and how he had caught it, holding her close to him by her hair.

She brushed harder, then she winced and stopped. At this rate she'd be scalping herself! When she went riding again she'd tie her hair back. She might try another style for everyday wear too.

But if she did Coll would think she was scared of her hair brushing him again. She wasn't, of course, but it was right what he said about enemies sharpening your senses. She could still feel his fingers in her hair.

It had been a good life before he came back, and she had thought she would be happy to go quietly on and marry Neil and live the quiet life. Well, the quiet life was out for the next six months, and she had enjoyed tonight. That midnight ride had been fantastic, she was still high on the thrill of it. Something inside her seemed to have woken again, as though she had been asleep for a long time.

She disliked Coll Sullivan, but working for him might be more stimulating than her dull job and her dull life with Neil. Perhaps she needed an enemy, a challenge. It was going to be a fight between them. If she lasted out the six months she had won, and remembering what the stakes were she daren't lose.

She felt strong and able to win, brushing her hair until it was smooth as silk again, then going to bed and putting on the alarm clock because it was almost two in the morning.

She wondered if Coll would oversleep up there in her home that was now his home, and which bedroom he was using. When she closed her eyes she remembered the rooms again, how they had been, how they were now, and in her dreams she walked through each, opening door after door quietly in the night.

She recalled her dream in her first waking moments, and wondered what she could have been seeking.

She had set the alarm for half past eight, but she woke just after seven and lay sleepily, going over her dream, trying to decide whether to get up or go to sleep again. Then she heard the car go by and thought —early start for Coll.

He was out of the way. The coast was clear, the house and the stables were all hers. That settled it; she got up, although while she was drinking coffee and making a piece of toast she reminded herself of her resolution never to make believe she was anything but a servant in the Manor House.

There were to be no daydreams. Coll Sullivan was owner and master and the old days would never come back. But Dora felt less depressed than yesterday when she walked up the drive, and she went to look at the horses before she went into the house.

Damozel came as soon as she opened the top of the stable door, as though greeting a friend, and that lightened Dora's heart. The hunter got to its feet, but it resisted her blandishments and stood well back and she laughed. 'Take your time, I'll be around for the next six months, and I'll be seeing to your breakfast if that groom doesn't turn up soon.'

She left the tops of the doors open and went looking

for her instructions, which she found where she had put the lists for Coll, on the counter in the hall.

He had signed the bottom of each typewritten page, with an occasional amendment. By 'Pictures' she had put a query, and he had written, 'All reproductions, all cheap. If any appeal to you hang on to them. Let the rest go.'

It shouldn't have been up to her to choose what hung on his walls, although they were going to look very bare if all the pictures went. Some of them were attractive, and if it was part of her job she'd do a selection. If he didn't approve he should have taken the trouble to make his own.

She turned to the handwritten notes. She had never seen his writing before, but she felt she might have guessed it would look the way it did: black, legible, strong and upright. It had the stamp of authority.

The groom would be arriving this morning and so would the pantechnicon. Dora was to supervise the removals and Coll would see her this evening about seven o'clock.

She said, 'That should keep me going for the day.'

Talking to herself, in a chirpy voice, made her feel less lonely. And now, as well as Tip, there were two horses outside, and a groom on his way, and a full schedule with the removal men.

Coll had written 'Excellent typing', referring to her lists, and she grimaced. What did he expect? That they would look as though she typed with her toes? She took a pen from her handbag and wrote, 'Thank you. We can't all be tycoons, but with practice we can all be typists.'

She was upstairs, checking the pictures again, when

Tip started to yap and then someone called, 'Miss Dora?'

'Tommy?' She hurried out of the bedroom on to the landing and along to the stairs, and was half way down when a man came into the hall from the kitchen passage.

He was middle height, with shoulders so broad they were out of proportion and arms a fraction too long. His physique, with a brown wrinkled face and hair that managed to look brown and wrinkled too, gave him the appearance of a small and amiable gorilla.

'I wondered if it might be you,' said Dora, and fled down the rest of the stairs to grab him like a long-lost friend. It wasn't that long since she had seen him, he lived in the village and did occasional work for a local riding school, but he had to be the groom Coll had told her was coming, because Tommy Corbett had been groom to the horses here in her father's day.

'Like old times, isn't it?' he said with a broad grin, and Dora made her own grin as wide.

'Yes,' she said, although that was never going to be true.

'They look all right.' He jerked his head in the direction of the stables—he meant the horses.

'They're super,' she agreed.

'You're getting the place straight, then?' Tommy must be in his late sixties now, but he had never seemed to change in all the years she had known him. He had taught her to ride, and when her father died and everything was sold Tommy, always a man of few words, had walked around as though he was shell-shocked, shaking his head, his world in ruins as well as theirs.

Dora asked, 'Do you remember Coll Sullivan?'

'A tinker lad, yes. He could ride.'

'What do you think of him now?'

Tommy grinned again, showing gappy teeth. 'He ain't a tinker any more, is he? Nice, somebody like that buying the old place. Putting horses back in the stables.'

'Mmm,' said Dora, and Tommy gave her a shrewd look.

'What brought him back here, then? You?'

'Goodness, *no*! He saw the house advertised and he wanted a house.' With the Holcrofts thrown in for good measure, they might have tipped the balance, but not—as Tommy thought—because he had liked them.

'Going to live in it, is he?' Tommy asked. 'Just him?'

'Yes.' She didn't know that for sure. He could be bringing people down, maybe the girl who rode the mare. 'He'll need a staff, of course,' she said.

'Like the old days.' Tommy liked the sound of that, he kept saying it. He looked around the hall. 'What about all this?' There had been no counter in the hall in the old days.

'It's being taken away,' Dora explained. 'Some men are coming today to move it all, and then there'll just be furniture, and it will look like a home again.'

'I'll go and see about the paddock,' said Tommy, satisfied.

She hadn't been in the paddock, but hawthorn hedges divided it from neighbouring fields, it should still be a secure place to let the horses run free. Tommy would soon have it secure if there were any gaps in the hedge or holes in the ground.

Dora had wondered if the groom might be Tommy, and she wondered who the rest of the staff would be,

Ten years had dispersed the rest, Dora had lost touch with all except the housekeeper, and she was housekeeping for her widower brother and his family in Lancashire, she wasn't looking for another job.

It was becoming exciting. She had expected to start all this 'putting back the clock' under a cloud of depression, but the challenge was charging her batteries, pepping up the adrenalin.

Half an hour later the removal men arrived, and from then on there was noise and clatter and bustle. and she had no time to think about anything except what she was doing.

It was easy enough to indicate the articles Coll didn't want, but there were fixtures to be taken down, and during the dismantling of the counter and shelves the air in the hall was thick with floating motes of dust.

In the middle of it all Thea phoned. The phone was on the floor, and Dora sat on the floor to answer, coughing as the dust hit her tonsils.

'What's happening?' asked Thea.

'They're taking the stuff away out of the hall.'

'Want any help?'

'I shouldn't bring Kiki into this, there's a lot of dust flying.' They were unscrewing the shelves away from the wall at that stage. 'Tell Simon Tommy's back,' said Dora, 'and there are two beautiful horses in the paddock.'

'We know,' said Thea. They would have seen Coll last night, but they didn't know Dora and Coll had been out riding. They couldn't have heard the horses clopping along in the quiet dark night. Dora opened her mouth to impart that bit of news, and Thea laughed.

'It's nice about Tommy,' she said, before Dora could speak, 'but I'm petrified of horses. A bike was more my style, and I gave them up when I went into long skirts.'

Dora began coughing again. 'We'll come along when the shop shuts,' said Thea, and left Dora coughing away.

When the removal men had gone the hall looked strange. The walls, where the shelves had been, would have to be redecorated, but she could do something about the pattern that the counter had left on the polished floor. She found dusters, a broom, a polishing mop, a tin of polish, and swept out the hall, then worked hard getting the shine back on the wooden blocks of the floor.

Tip had been fastened up most of the day. He was small and lively and could easily have slipped under someone's feet. If the someone had been furniture removing at the time there could have been a mighty crash, so Dora had shut him in a small downstairs room in which he had passed the time either sleeping or yapping.

He came shooting out, and investigated busily for a few minutes. Then he stretched out on the bottom step of the staircase and watched Dora cleaning the hall.

After a while Tommy came in. 'Well, Miss Dora,' he said, 'I never thought to see this.' This was Dora, on her knees, polishing the floor; and that made her smile because it was a long time since anyone had done her housework. Tommy must know that. She had seen him from time to time in the last ten years. He knew she worked for her living, and lived alone, just as he knew that the 'young master' ran a shop. But back here, in the Manor House, he was astonished to find 'Miss Dora' getting her dainty little hands dirty.

She said, 'I work here now.'

'That's all right, but—scrubbing floors!'

'Polishing, actually, although it could do with scrubbing. How about getting us another cup of tea?'

It was mouth-drying work, cleaning up, although the house hadn't been empty long. Another day or so, perhaps the help of another strong-armed woman, and Dora would have the place clean. She had enjoyed today, and she went into the kitchen to drink her tea with Tommy.

He had been groom here for the best years of his life. He remembered her father with affection and the firm belief that someone had cheated Laurence Holcroft out of the Manor House and all that went with it.

No one had. He had cheated himself. But Tommy still thought he was king and Dora had to listen to rambling tales that stirred sad memories for her.

But it wasn't unbearable. She managed to smile at Tommy's racier accounts, and when he said, 'And we're back here now, who'd have thought that'd ever happen,' she said,

'So we are.' She had never thought to be back, and she had to wait until Simon arrived and told her what kind of contract he had signed with Coll before she would know what price she was expected to pay.

When she read the copy of the contract that evening she read that it was up to her. That was what it came down to, as she had already been told. If she walked out the loan could be called in.

'I suppose I can now describe myself as a rich man's whim,' she said. 'It sounds Victorian, doesn't it? Fair but frail.'

Simon hooted. 'Frail? You? You're tough as old boots.'

'Right, brother,' she said, and wondered if that was true, and wondered what would happen to her if it wasn't. She said, in a broad country accent, 'Anyhow, maister'll be 'ome about seven,' and reverted to her own voice. 'And I'm through my first day, so I've only got about another hundred and seventy-nine to go.'

Tommy pedalled off on his cranky old bike before Coll came. It was only 'family' in the kitchen, and Coll came in as though he had been doing this for years, and always finding them waiting for him. He was elegant in city clothes against Simon's country tweeds, and Dora felt particularly dishevelled.

Thea had brought food again and Coll walked around eating a ham and lettuce sandwich, looking at the gaps where the hotel furniture used to be, deciding with Simon and Thea how they were going to be filled.

Dora deliberately kept her opinions to herself. In any case she agreed with the suggestions that were coming up. It would be super if the house could develop along those lines. It would be a lovely home again.

They went out to the stables, Simon and Dora and Coll. Thea stayed where she could hear Kiki if the baby woke up, and as she told them all again, she wasn't enthusiastic about horses. 'Too *big*,' she said. 'I like little furry animals,' and she patted Tip.

'I'll be away for the next fortnight,' Coll said when the three of them were in the courtyard. 'I'd be glad if you'd exercise the horses.'

'You bet!' grinned Simon.

'We'd like that,' said Dora. So he wouldn't be here for two whole weeks. She would be nominally in charge and she would like that too. 'What are my duties while you're away?'

'Your duties.' Coll turned that smile on her. 'That sounds very subservient.'

'What do you expect me to do to earn my salary?' she said shortly, because that hadn't amused her.

'Get the house ready. Interview the staff.'

'What staff?'

'How many do I need to run this place?'

They were standing around Loki's stable door, Coll was stroking his neck and the great dark head turned as though it was following the conversation.

'We had a housekeeper, didn't we?' Simon recalled. 'One girl who lived in and another who used to come in from the village, a gardener and Tommy.'

'Ever tried hiring domestic staff these days?' said Dora to Coll.

'No, but I've never found any difficulty in getting service. Have you?'

'Of course I haven't hired anybody.' He knew that.

'Do your best,' he said. 'If you can't manage it I'll deal with the problem when I get back.'

'What wages do I offer?' He told her and she nodded. She'd get a staff together. If she couldn't find resident help she'd find local, who wanted work for the hours while the children were at school. She was supposed to be the housekeeper, and it suddenly became a matter of personal pride to her that the house should be smoothly run.

As they walked back across the courtyard it was Simon who asked, 'Are you going to live here on your own?'

'I'll have guests coming down.'

'Girl-friends?' said Dora. Not that it was of any

interest to her, she just asked for something to say.

'Probably.'

'Anyone in particular?' She looked at him with cool amusement as they walked into the house.

'Yes.'

'What's she like?' Not that Dora cared, again she was just talking, and Coll sounded surprised and amused.

'Not unlike you to look at, but that's where the resemblance ends.'

'I've often thought there are a lot of women who look like me,' she said.

Simon went seeking Thea, who was in the room where Kiki was sleeping. As she walked into the kitchen Dora asked, 'Doesn't she mind you trying to seduce other women?'

'No.'

'Funny girl!'

She went to the table and began to gather food together. She didn't know if Thea wanted to take the remains home with her, or if they could stay here. She could feel Coll's eyes on her, all the time, and she didn't want to look at him.

But she did. She glanced across to where he was standing, and met a look of such direct intensity that she couldn't turn her head away again. She had to stare back.

She had a terrifying feeling of being on the edge of a precipice, with a roaring in her ears, poised to fall into some maelstrom from which there could be no escape.

He said softly, 'It will happen.'

He meant that he would be her lover. 'No!' she whispered. She didn't hear Simon and Thea until they were in the room beside her, although they had come laughing and talking along the corridor.

Simon and Thea and Dora, and Kiki—and Tip, of course—all left together. It had been a pleasant evening; Coll was urbane and charming and Simon looked years younger because he had Coll's cheque in the bank, and Coll's commission to find the furniture that the house would be needing.

Dora was in bed, trying to sleep, when she heard the soft clop-clop of hooves on the gravel. She had gone straight to bed as soon as she got home, and she was glad the lodge was in darkness in case he might have come for her. Tonight she could not have gone riding.

But there was no check in the rhythm of the hooves and she listened, holding her breath, as the black hunter went by.

During the next two weeks Dora was constantly surprised to find herself feeling so happy. She knew that too much contentment was foolish, but it was good to be in the old house again, helping Simon and Thea arrange the new pieces of furniture. She waited for the purchases to arrive, so excited that she was dancing around the rooms like a sixteen-year-old.

She got staff locally. She got the man who had worked as gardener while the Manor was a guesthouse, and a woman who had helped with the cleaning. Until she knew what kind of entertaining Coll planned to do she could probably handle the cooking herself.

She was busy from morning till night. She worked in the house and the garden. Sometimes early morning, sometimes in the evening, she and Simon rode on the heath, and every day was a challenge and an achievement. At the end of every day she felt that the house looked a little better.

She couldn't put Coll completely out of her mind. He was the pivot of everything that was happening. He was abroad, but accounts had to be prepared for when he came back. They had to abide by his rules. He had told them to employ domestic help, to exercise the horses, to buy what they were buying. But sometimes she pretended she was pleasing herself.

One thing she decided was to stay in the house overnight. The staff all lived out, and there were several items now that might tempt a thief. A house that was empty by night was asking for trouble, and a girl and a barking dog were better than no guards at all.

She would go back to the lodge to sleep as soon as Coll returned, but while he was out of the country she did feel responsible.

By habit she chose the room she had slept in until she was seventeen, but there was nothing familiar left in there. When she woke in the mornings she had to get out of bed and look out of the window, or walk into the corridor, before she felt as though she was back in the Manor.

If she lay awake at night she had to close her eyes, shutting out the faint shadowy shape of the furnishings, and then the sounds of the house brought her comfort and a sense of security.

But the night Tip's yapping woke her she sat up feeling very insecure. She looked out of the window and there was light streaming over from one of the garages, so this was no burglar. It was Coll come home.

They had expected him back tonight, but he had rung earlier in the day to say that he might not make it until tomorrow. They had waited, the three of them, with a meal ready, and then eaten most of the meal, then Simon and Thea had left, and Dora had hung around until past midnight.

She should have gone home, even when she thought it was certain Coll wouldn't be back. But she had thought the house was going to be empty again, and she had come upstairs to bed, intending to be up early in the morning.

She got dressed as though the house was on fire, flinging on a quick covering. She didn't want him tracking the sound of Tip's yaps to her bedroom door.

The lights were on downstairs now, and at the top of the stairs she called 'Hello!' then realised that if this *was* a break-in she had done just about the silliest thing possible. But thieves wouldn't go around switching on the lights. Would they?

'Hello,' Coll came into the hall, and Tip trotted down to welcome him, followed, slower and with less enthusiasm, by Dora. 'What are you doing here?' he asked her.

'Guarding the property.'

'*My* property?' He was going to laugh at that, and she explained,

'Simon and Thea have been unloading some quite valuable stuff here since you went away. If anyone had swiped that would you have paid up?'

He grinned. 'And you've been guarding it? Who else is here?'

'Nobody.'

'No, staff?'

She was at the bottom of the stairs now. 'Not living in,' she said.

'So you're living in?'

'Not now you're back. Shall I get you something to eat?'

'Thank you.' He followed her into the kitchen, where she made tea and brought out some cold meat and pickles, and told him about the staff situation and what Simon had bought on his behalf.

Coll listened, nodding assent as though it was all satisfactory. He didn't look tired, the handsome hawk-ish face was smooth as ever, but he probably was, and if it had been anyone else Dora would have poured out his tea and urged him to eat up and get to bed.

He poured his own tea, and said, 'You're not joining me, of course?'

She didn't want to stay here tonight a minute longer than she must. She said, 'No, thanks, I'll be getting along home.'

'Leaving me to deal with the thieves?'

'You'll be all right,' she said. 'You——' Afterwards she couldn't remember what she would have said then. It wouldn't have been provocative, because she cer-tainly wasn't looking for a showdown at this time of night. But she forgot for ever what she had been going to say when he asked, in the tone of casual conversa-tion,

'Talking of thieves, did you ever find those pearls of yours?'

She was stung to fury. She said hotly, 'You know I didn't. You took them.'

'No,' he said.

Of course he was denying it. Of course he would, especially now he was Sullivan Properties. He wouldn't want it known he had been a thief. She could never prove it after all these years, but she couldn't endure him taunting her, jeering about it. Any time he brought up the subject she'd tell him again that she knew him for what he was.

L

'You're lying,' she said.

'I rarely lie,' he drawled. 'I rarely find the need.'

He got up suddenly, pulled out a chair from the table, gripped her arms and sat her down as unceremoniously as though she was a large rag doll.

'Have some supper, Dora-Lily,' he said. 'And we'll finish that conversation we started ten years ago over breakfast.'

CHAPTER SEVEN

DORA'S breath seemed shaken out of her. She could only sit there gasping, shaking her head when he asked, 'Do you want a cup of tea?'

He sat down, facing her across the table, no tension in his loose limbs. 'I don't really care whether you believe this or not,' he said, 'but I never saw your bloody pearls after you walked out of the room that night.'

He would deny it, of course he would, but he sounded so convincing. He was looking straight at her, and she felt a blush starting in her cheeks as though she was the guilty one.

'I came here that day to see you both,' he went on quietly. 'I was starting to get my life together and I thought you might like to know.'

His hands were clasped, the fingers locked. He sat easily with an athlete's grace, but Dora couldn't take her eyes off his hands on the table. They were so tight clenched that she felt he was clenching them to keep them off her. That in spite of the quiet voice he wanted to hit out.

She couldn't speak, she couldn't move. She sat still, listening to him. 'It made no difference to you that I wasn't a tinker any longer. When you mislaid your pearls you couldn't wait to accuse me. You must have run every inch of the way. You'd got as much colour in your face as you've got now.'

Her blush deepened. She could feel it creeping to her hairline and she managed to gasp huskily, 'Why didn't you deny it?'

'Why should I?' he shot back at her. 'You had no proof, just your nasty suspicious little mind. I didn't care who searched or questioned me. You were the one who would have looked the fool.'

She had realised that, but why hadn't he said something to stop her carrying on? He gave a sudden harsh laugh. 'You badly wanted to call the police, didn't you? If you could have seen me led handcuffed away it would have been worth losing your pearls. You were a vindictive little devil.'

Dora remembered her anger that morning, the sick futility of it all. Her mother's pearls and Coll laughing. It had all been so horrible that she had never told anyone else what had happened.

No one else had noticed that she didn't have her pearls. Her father had other things on his mind for his few remaining months of life, and she had let Simon believe she had accepted the explanation that she had lost them herself. She said dully, 'I never found them.'

Coll shrugged. 'You were going to a party, weren't you?'

'I went riding instead. On my own.'

She hadn't even bothered to saddle the horse. She had ridden bareback in her party dress, galloping off like a gipsy. Perhaps she should have been the tinker's child, not Coll. If she had worn the pearls, and they had slipped off, they could have fallen into the rough grasses of the heath and stayed hidden for ever. Or have been picked up any time in the last ten years.

For the first time she was really wondering, 'Did I wear them?'

'I don't know.' Her uncertainty was ten years too late, but he remembered, 'You were trying to fasten them.'

'Yes.' She had stood in front of a mirror, fumbling with the catch. 'It was faulty,' she said, 'the fastener.'

She had been so prejudiced against Coll, and yet she had never known him take anything that didn't belong to him. So why had she gone running to accuse him?

It must have been because she wanted to believe the worst about him. She *had* wanted to see him humiliated. Like he said, she would have clapped him into handcuffs if she had had the power. She must have hated him.

He remembered that morning and her asking if his father was in jail. He must hate her, and she said unsteadily, 'I was so sure.'

'You always were,' he drawled.

It was her father who should have been in jail, not his. Her childhood had been protected, but when she was sixteen and Coll was twenty her days of security were numbered. She said, 'I shouldn't have been. I really had nothing.'

An apology would be meaningless in the present circumstances, all the same she said, 'I wish you'd said this then.'

'What difference would it have made then?' he asked. 'You'd better get to bed. I'll be off at eight in the morning and I'd like some breakfast before I go.'

'Of course.' She was tired, her sleep had been disturbed and she was drained emotionally as well as physically. 'I'll go home,' she said.

'Oh, go to bed.' Coll sounded weary for the first time. 'Double-bar your door if you think you're that irresistible after one hell of a day.'

She didn't. She didn't want to walk down the drive to the lodge either. She said, 'All right. Goodnight.'

She undressed again and got into bed again, and lay wondering why she was suddenly convinced that she had been mistaken all these years. There was no doubt in her mind now that she had worn her pearls and lost them, and little doubt that Coll Sullivan was going to make her pay for the way she had treated him.

She must be up at seven to see about breakfast, and if she was going to wake she must get to sleep. She had slept easier in the big old house when she had been alone, the thought of him so near disturbed her, and when she did fall asleep she dreamt that dream again, where she walked in the darkness, on silent bare feet, opening door after door ...

At half past seven she wondered whether she should be waking him up. She knew the room he used. It had clothes in the wardrobe and drawers, aftershave in the adjoining bathroom.

She took up a cup of tea and tapped on the door, and he opened it. He was dressed, except for tie and jacket, his hair slightly ruffled. 'Thanks,' he said, taking the cup of tea. 'How are you going to provide this every morning at this hour unless you're living in?'

'I'm going to walk the two minutes from my house,' she said.

'Are you scared to sleep in my house?'

'Why should I worry? What could you do to me?'

She managed to sound scoffing, and he grinned.

'A number of things.' His eyes travelled up and down her, lingering on lips and breasts like a touch, and Dora had a wild surmise that he was about to draw her through the open door into the room where he had passed the night, to the bed from which he had just risen.

She didn't stop to consider how he could carry her unwillingly to bed when he was holding a full cup of tea. She set off down the corridor, asking as she went, 'What do you want for breakfast? The cooked menu? Bacon? Eggs?' and stopped at a prudent distance for his reply.

'Coffee and toast.'

'You could have got that for yourself.'

'I don't like eating breakfast alone.'

'You could always get Tommy in.'

'No, thanks.'

She went on her way smiling, in spite of everything, and when Coll came into the kitchen five minutes later she was sitting at the table. 'You look good in the mornings,' he observed.

Dora poured two coffees, 'But not so bright at night?'

'From what I've seen of you, not bad at all.'

'Splendid,' she said, and handed him his coffee, 'because what you've seen of me is all you're going to see.'

He grinned and she grinned back. It was when the laughing stopped that the hurting might start, and this was a man with the power to harm.

She produced the toast and said, 'This isn't much for starters, especially if you're expecting another hellish day.'

'What?' He looked up from buttering, and she reminded him,

'You said yesterday had been a hell of a day.'

'Did I?' He seemed to have forgotten. 'A long one. But I'll have you to come back to tonight.'

'I was here last night.' She sat down again, sipping her coffee.

'But it had been a long day, so it was a short night,' he said, and she pulled a face.

'I can see you don't have many breakfasts alone, with such a practised line in patter!'

'You've cooked many breakfasts, have you?' he enquired, and when she looked blank, 'for the three you nearly married.'

'Actually,' she drawled, 'they used to cook breakfast for me.' Coll laughed,

'I can believe that,' although he shouldn't have done, none of them had ever stayed for breakfast. 'Can you cook?' he asked.

'I'm a smashing cook.' This wasn't an ideal kitchen for a private house, it had been designed for a guesthouse, but she had done enough practising in the past fortnight to work out the most economic way of using the equipment. 'What time do you want dinner?'

'About eight o'clock.'

'Anything in particular?'

'Surprise me,' he invited.

'Just you?'

'And you.'

Dora looked as though she was thinking about that, and she was but she wasn't going to be allowed much say in the matter. 'Is it part of the job?' she enquired.

'Yes. Ask Simon and Thea to come for a meal at the weekend. Tonight there'll be just the two of us.'

'Will there?' she said coolly. 'I hope I'm going to be allowed some social life while I work for you.'

'I'll keep you amused.' He went on with his breakfast and she said,

'I'm sure you will. But not by imagining you've got *droit de seigneur.*'

He chuckled. 'I thought that was reserved for virgins.'

'That,' she said flippantly, 'was what they told the *seigneur*. It was the only choice the girl had. She could keep her mouth shut and let the lord of the manor think he was first.'

'You prefer to choose your own lovers?' He looked up with a gleam of dark eyes and she said emphatically.

'I most certainly do!'

'But this time you're being hunted,' and the gleam was wholly predatory, 'so where will you run?'

'I don't run,' she said briskly. 'I fight.'

'This is going to be worth the money.' He was laughing and she said,

'How kind of you to say so.'

He got up. 'Right, I'm off.' He reached for her hand and kissed her palm swiftly. 'I'll see you this evening.'

'Probably.' Dora didn't move. She stayed there, sipping her coffee, listening to a door close and the car drive away. When there was no sound at all but the ticking of the kitchen clock the kiss was still tingling to her fingertips.

She went upstairs and made the bed in the room she had been using. She wouldn't be sleeping in here again unless she was absolutely sure that Coll would not be returning. There wasn't much that belonged to her, only her nightdress, a dressing gown, and the toilet articles she stuffed into a small overnight case.

She would take that home when she went shopping.

Then she went to his room. The heavy old doors had brass knobs and creaked slightly when the knob was turned and the door was pushed; and Dora hesitated, peering in, as though Coll might not have left in that car after all.

The room had been neat and unused for the past fortnight, but now it seemed warm, alive, with a robe thrown over a chair, and the sheets thrown back from the bed.

She hung up the robe and made the bed. There didn't seem to be any pyjamas about. She smoothed the pillow with a light lingering touch, and then the coverlet, almost as though someone lay beneath it. A man with long limbs and hard muscles.

Physically, of course, he was attractive. In every other way he was impossible, and he had a rock bottom opinion of her. A vindictive little devil who had grown into a woman who hadn't changed much. That was what he had said, 'You haven't changed much either.'

But if things had been different, and she had been looking for a lover, she might have looked twice at him. Maybe, even, more than twice.

She went quickly out of the room, and found plenty to occupy herself downstairs until Tommy arrived, and then Mrs Heaton the daily. As Dora left the air was humming with the noise of Mrs Heaton's vacuum cleaner, and Tommy was whistling shrilly while he cleaned out the stables. It all sounded busy and cheerful.

So did Thea when Dora collected her to go shopping for provisions in town. Simon and Thea were both blooming these days. Dora had always thought they both looked fine before Coll came, but she could see now how some of the strain had slipped away. They looked as though they had just returned from a good holiday.

Simon was left minding the shop, Kiki was secured in the back seat of the Mini with Tip on the floor, and Thea took the passenger seat by Dora.

'Coll turned up last night,' said Dora, as they drove away. 'Very late, but we had a talk. You remember me telling you about my mother's pearls?'

'I'm not likely to have forgotten that, am I?' said Thea.

Dora said quietly, 'I think now that I did go out wearing them. I think they slipped off.'

'What changed your mind?' Thea was looking very hard at her.

'Coll did. Last night. When it happened I accused him of taking them and he laughed and said—prove it. But last night he said that he didn't take them, and I think I believe him.'

Thea sank back in her seat, giving a soft happy little laugh. 'Well, that's all right, then. I'm so glad you've cleared that up, because that was really all you'd got against him, wasn't it?'

No, it wasn't. He had always disrupted everything. Dora had always been a little scared of what he might do. But the pearls had been the bitterest part. It was the thought of that last morning that festered and, once she admitted to herself that she had misjudged him there, she had to change some of her opinions.

But he didn't. Nothing had changed for him and nothing would amuse him more than to strip her of her pride. So she must be very careful not to give him the chance.

To begin with she would be so efficient that he'd

have no grounds for complaint about her work. She shopped, thriftily but with imaginative flair, so that she could provide delicious meals, and coming up to eight o'clock that night she had dinner waiting.

Tommy and Mrs Heaton had gone and Dora had prepared spiced lamb chops with some attractively assorted vegetables, then changed into a bright pink cotton dress which was pretty and cool after the hot kitchen work.

She heard the car arrive and went to the back door, then turned and hurried into the drawing room and picked up a newspaper. She was on duty, but she didn't want to give the impression she had been hovering behind the door, ready to open it obsequiously when the master arrived.

Tip yapped, of course, and Coll called from the hall, 'Dora-Lily!'

'I'm here.' As he came through the door she put aside her newspaper and said, 'The meal's ready, everything's in hand—and please will you stop calling me Dora-Lily?'

'Not so easy, when that's how I've thought of you all these years.'

She shifted uncomfortably before his ironic gaze. She was pretending to be at home here, in the drawing room, but even the chair she sat on belonged to him.

She said, 'I doubt if you've thought of me at all in all these years.'

'From time to time. You said yourself there are an awful lot of girls who look like you.'

She had said that, but it was no compliment to hear she belonged in the crowd, she would rather be told she was a special enemy. She asked, 'Do you want this meal?'

'Can I wash and change first?'

He came down in the thin grey polo-necked sweater and grey slacks he had worn when he arrived at Simon's shop less than a month ago, and took his seat, and Dora served up the meal.

Coll said it was good, which it was; then he asked a few questions and she told him how she had passed her day and said, 'I'd like to be doing some secretarial work. I don't want to get so out of practice that I can't get another job at the end of my six months. Will you bring work home?'

'Yes.' He went on with his eating. 'But most of it's confidential and I'm not sure how far I can trust you. You're here for the money. Suppose you were offered more money to sell me out?'

If he was serious she was furious that he should think her dishonest. But she had accused him of stealing, so she bit her lip and said drily, 'Industrial spying, you mean? How do I go about selling the secrets? Avertise?'

'If you get any you could try a line in the *Financial Times*.'

They both began to laugh at the ridiculous notion of her doing a Mata Hari through his briefcase, and after the meal she took down some dictation—being tested, she felt.

Coll dictated fast. He knew exactly what he wanted to say and how to say it. But Dora was up to the speed and when he asked, 'Do you think you could get that typed out tomorrow?' she said airily,

'Of course.'

'You have a typewriter?'

'Yes.' She yawned a little, emphasising the time, and he asked solicitously,

'Ready for bed?'

'For my own bed. I'm going home.'

He sighed. 'Still as stubborn.'

'I wasn't stubborn,' she protested. She closed her notebook with a snap. She had been spoilt as a child, but she hadn't been particularly obstinate. Except with him. He *was* the only enemy she had ever had. She said, 'You always brought out the worst in me. I was much nicer when you weren't around. Can I go home now?'

Coll looked at her impassively. 'You never feel that you are at home?' and she wondered if he meant that to hurt. She said,

'But I'm not. I'll be back to cook your breakfast.'

'Thank you,' he said, and she walked home alone, which was how she wanted it.

She did some quiet thinking next day as she typed out the notes he had dictated to her, gleaning faint glimmerings of the extent of his business acumen and enterprise. By any standards Coll was exceptional, cleverer and tougher than anyone else she knew.

Maybe that was what had bothered her about him as a child. He must have been born with the one-in-a-million mind and the thrusting drive. Her friends had all been nice ordinary children. When Dora was among them she was always in the lead. She was smarter, and she could ride faster and swim farther than most of them. Simon was four years her senior, but she had always felt stronger than Simon. She had never let him or Thea suspect that, but she had. The only real competition in her childhood had come from Coll.

Those rare times when he was around she had been restless; even as a child she had always wanted to outrace him. During that sports day, years and years ago, when she had watched him doing all the winning, her frustration had not been because he was outstripping Simon and the other boys, but because she couldn't be in the race herself. She wouldn't have had a hope of winning, but she had yearned passionately to challenge him, and now she hadn't a hope of outracing him in anything.

She went on with her typing, concentrating so that she made no mistakes, not a single one. 'O.K., Mr Sullivan,' she said to the empty room, as she collected the completed pages together, 'try doing better than that!'

Coll was around for the weekend. Both days he and Dora went riding, and as they galloped over the heath on Sunday morning she called, 'Can I ride Loki?'

'Of course,' he called back, 'when I'm not riding him.'

She had, but she wanted to change horses now. 'I meant now,' she said, and he laughed as though he was reading her thoughts.

'I'm not having you on the faster horse. You might get away.'

'I can't get away,' she said glumly. 'I've been sold into slavery.'

She was something of a slave in the weeks that followed. She worked very long hours, although the work wasn't all that arduous.

She did secretarial work and she ran the house, and it was a never-failing thrill when Simon and Thea came up with something new that was usually something old. They found several antique pieces and some good reproductions, and the Manor was becoming a home again.

Guests came occasionally and Dora organised the hospitality. No obvious girl-friend turned up, and it was embarrassing to know that everybody who came to the Manor presumed that Dora and Coll were having an affair. She was more or less living in his house and it wasn't the kind of thing she could issue denial statements about. It was the local belief as well, and the more she tried to play down the impression the more firmly entrenched it became. At the end of her second month of working for Coll she bumped into Mrs Hewitt in town, who enquired acidly when the wedding was to be.

'What wedding?' asked Dora, and Mrs Hewitt gave her a pinched smile.

'Of course not,' said Mrs Hewitt. 'Why should the young man marry you when he's enjoying all the advantages of matrimony with none of the responsibilities?'

'They all think I'm the mistress of the Manor,' said Dora, reporting this to Thea. 'Nobody believes I'm just a skivvy. I don't know why I bother to preserve my virtue.'

'If you ask me,' said Thea, 'neither do I. I suppose you haven't——' she paused, and Dora snapped,

'No, I have *not*!'

'Strong-minded old you,' teased Thea, and she didn't know how right she was.

Coll's propositioning was constant, delivered with a light touch and a charm that kept it from being objectionable. He wanted Dora. She knew that he didn't much like her, but one day—either from exhaustion or because she was laughing and didn't quite realise what was going on—he confidently expected her to fall into his arms.

Well, she wouldn't. They skirmished all the time, and there were occasions when Dora glimpsed the darker side of his nature, sensing coldness, cruelty that reinforced her instincts of self-preservation.

She worked for him and with him. She was his constant companion, sometimes far into the night. But if she ever let him get too close, herself without covering or protection, she felt that he might stab her to the heart...

One early evening, in late October, he looked up from a letter she had typed for him and said, 'We should be celebrating.'

'Celebrating what?'

There was a beautiful bow-fronted walnut desk now in the library. Dora had an electric typewriter on it. She was sitting there and Coll was standing beside her, the letter in his hands. He said, 'It's three months since we met again, and you haven't poisoned me and I haven't seduced you, don't you think that's something to celebrate? Let's go out to dinner.'

She had a casserole prepared for dinner, but an evening out would be pleasant. 'Of course it is,' she said. 'Where shall we go?'

'You go and change, I'll ring around.'

Dora hurried home to the lodge and picked out a long white crocheted dress. There was a nip of autumn in the air, but if she wore it with a black silk-fringed shawl she should be warm enough. She made up with a quick and practised hand, adding an extra glow and sheen, and was waiting when the car drew up in the drive.

Tip trotted along beside her. She took him around with her these days, he dozed happily in any car and Coll didn't seem to mind. Tip slipped in before Dora, wriggling his way into the back seat, and it was something to be driving in a super car with a handsome man. It was a nice way to round off a busy day.

Everyone looked at them when they arrived. Waiters and diners, especially the women, always looked at Coll. He was in black pants and a dark green velvet jacket, and his shirt and tie were silk. He looked dashing and distinguished, and Dora watched him discussing the menu with the waiter and the wine waiter, agreeing when she was consulted. She was hungry, she had skimped on meals today because she had been busy, and the suggestions sounded mouth-watering.

When the waiters walked away Coll looked across at her, catching her pensive air, asking, 'What are you thinking about?'

She had been remembering that her father had once brought her here, it was an old-established eating spot not far from home. He had ordered wine, pouring half a glass for her, drinking the rest of the bottle himself. She said, 'My father, we came here together once.'

Her father had liked her to be pretty and feminine, with the graces of a well-born young lady. She wondered now how she would have turned out if life had gone on the way it had been in her childhood, and realised that she would have been very bored, she preferred working for her living.

Coll's father had died too and she asked him, 'If your father had lived would you have stayed with him.'

'No.' It was a silly question, of course he wouldn't have stayed in the trailer. 'But I would have seen that things were right for him.' Of course he would, but as she wondered how close the bond had been between the father who was a loser and the son who was born to win he added quietly, 'I loved him.'

'I loved my father too.' Dora spoke just as quietly, and he smiled,

'You see, we do have something in common,' the smile widened to a grin, 'which was more than our fathers did.'

Both men had been losers, but that wasn't what he meant, and she asked him something she had wondered about ever since he came back. 'How did you start? I know you bought that old barn, but what happened to you between fourteen and twenty?'

'They put me in a home for twelve months.' That must have been grim for a boy who had been on the open road all his life, but he didn't sound resentful. He explained, 'I wasn't hurt in the smash-up. Nor was the bloody fool who ran into us, only my father.'

There was resentment in that, but it was resigned, tempered by the years. 'It was a kids' home,' he went on. 'Not bad at all. I learned a lot while I was there. When I left I started working on a building site.'

The first course was being served. Coll picked up a fork in a manicured hand. 'You might not believe this,' he said, 'but I'm a twenty-brick man with a hod.'

His hands were strong. Under that silk shirt and velvet coat muscles rippled. 'That sounds a lot of bricks,' Dora commented.

'So I made some money. And I saved and I bought and I sold.'

That summed it up and told her nothing. She said, 'If it isn't a cheek asking, where did you pick up the polish? I mean, you're better educated than Simon and me, aren't you?'

And not just in practical things. Academically as well. He spoke French, German, and Spanish fluently.

Except for antiques, in which subject Simon had been immersed for the past ten years, Coll seemed to know more than Simon and Dora about almost everything.

He shrugged. 'Perhaps I pick up things faster than you and Simon.' He gave that a wry double meaning, and Dora knew it was a crack about the pearls and she said,

'Please, no. I lost them. I know I lost them.'

'We might go looking for them some day.'

'The string will have rotted,' she said, smiling wryly herself. 'They'll all have rolled away.'

'Never mind.' The wine had arrived and their glasses were filled. It was delicious and she was thirsty. She sipped it appreciatively, and Coll began to tell her about his time on the building site and his early days as a tyro tycoon. His clawing climb from rags to riches was fascinating and funny, and related with a self-mocking gaiety that would have disarmed anyone.

It disarmed Dora. She had reached the half way house of her six months' journey comparatively un-scathed, and she relaxed. She was entitled to an evening out and it was super to laugh without care, not feeling for once that beneath the surface Coll despised and disliked her.

She liked him tonight. He was putting himself out to entertain, and this was a superb meal. He had his good points. He had been very generous to Simon and Thea, and there had been nothing mean about his treatment of herself.

She put her hand over her wineglass, suddenly feeling that perhaps he had been a shade over-generous with the wine. She hadn't noticed how much she was drinking. She wasn't much of a drinker, but it had been sharp and sparkling and refreshing, and she said now, 'No more.'

'Sure?'

'Very sure.' She blinked, the lights and everyone else blurred a little, and she said, concerned, 'And you're driving.'

But Coll wasn't blinking. He was blurred, but not blinking, and she glared at him accusingly. 'You haven't drunk nearly as much as me.'

He was driving and he had the sense to know when to stop. 'I've been doing most of the talking,' he said.

She was glad the coffee in her cup was black. She drank it to the dregs and said, 'I think you'd better get me home.'

Coll was amused, looking at her as though he was trying not to smile. He had been pouring the stuff, and keeping her laughing and listening so that she hadn't noticed how much she was drinking, and she had better go very carefully indeed for the remainder of the evening.

He signalled to the waiter and Dora walked out, very carefully, feeling better for the fresh air, gulping it in all the way to the car. In the car Coll turned to look at her. 'Sure you're all right?'

'Yes. I'm a little light in the head, but if I can keep the window down I shall be perfectly fine.'

She knew she was muzzy, but she was more relaxed than she had ever been in his company, almost in a party mood and sorry that the evening was reaching its end. She would have liked to go dancing or, failing that, walking in the moonlight and the lovely cool air.

There was a splendid moon, a great golden orb, shedding a pale golden light over everything. The car was very comfortable, but the shining world outside seemed more inviting.

Dora sat with the wind in her hair, watching the night glide by, and when they came to a place she had always liked she asked, 'Would you stop for a minute?'

Coll braked at once, drawing into the lane that turned from the busier road. He leaned swiftly across and opened her door before his, but he was round to her side of the car before she had swung her feet out.

She got out and stood up. He thought she was feeling ill, but she was feeling fine. She said, 'I'd like to walk down to the river. Would you mind walking down to the river? You remember the river here, don't you?'

It was the weir stretch where the water flowed faster and the currents became dangerous. It was where he had dived in one day and called to Simon to follow him. For once Simon hadn't. Simon had never swum from this spot, but there was a time when Dora had come swimming here, alone.

Now, humming a little tune, accompanied by a silent Coll, she walked down the winding lane to the field and across to the river. Tip peered over at the dark water when they reached it, then backed hastily, and Coll put a hand on Dora's arm and said, 'I wouldn't advise it for sobering up. Too drastic.'

She was filled with a wild mischievous gaiety. 'Fancy finding ourselves here,' she gurgled. 'Do you believe in coincidence?'

'Why?'

'You swam across just here and called to Simon.' She shook off his restraining hand and walked along on the very edge. 'I wanted to dive in,' she said, 'I was a better swimmer than Simon, but I wasn't sure then that I could do it.' The night breeze lifted her shawl like black wings. 'I practised after that,' she said. 'I swam and swam, because one day I wanted to swim as well as you. Or better. But you never came down here with us again.'

She turned to face him. He was very close beside her. 'I bet I could race you to the other side!' Her voice was shrill with glee like a child's, and Coll was amused and tolerant as he might have been at a child showing off.

'And what do we do when we get to the other side?'

'Swim back again.'

'But of course.'

'But you don't think I'll do it?'

He shook his head slowly. 'Not in that dress.'

'No problem,' she said blithely. She dropped the black silk shawl, languid as a strip artist, and wriggled out of the long white crocheted dress, leaving herself in bra, pants and underskirt.

Coll stood with folded arms, smiling at her. 'Much more of that and you'll get pneumonia without having to swim for it.'

She knew then that she would have dived off a cliff to take the grin off his face. She dived into the river, a neat shallow dive that hardly made a splash. The cold took her breath for a moment, but when she surfaced she got out a line she badly wanted to say. 'Come on in, the water's lovely.'

'Come back, you little fool!' he roared, but she went on swimming away from him. The currents were trickiest mid-stream. You got into the undertow there, the pull of the weir making itself felt, but she knew that she could get across because she had before, even if it was over ten years ago. She was an even stronger swimmer now.

She looked back and Coll was kicking off his shoes, dragging off his coat, as though she was going down for the third time. She floated for a moment and he came up beside her, dark hair smooth and wet, moonlight shining on his face, white teeth bared in what looked like a smile but wasn't, because he was snarling, 'Get back to the bank!'

'I'm getting to the other side,' she said, and he caught her floating hair and said, as though he meant it,

'If you don't swim back I'll flaming well drown you!'

He was going to tow her back, whether she wanted to go or not, so she turned around. 'First thing in the morning,' she said as he loosed her, 'I'm going to get my hair cropped. I'm fed up being grabbed by my hair.'

She swam back in a strong swift crawl and he swam beside her, hauling himself out, then reaching for her, but she was scrambling out unaided. As she did she said, 'Don't glare at me, I didn't push you in.'

She pulled her dress over her head, clamping her clammy underclothes to her skin, putting her wet feet into her shoes. She was warm at the moment, but she was going to start shivering soon.

'We must have a proper race some time,' she said gaily. 'I always wanted to beat you.'

'Try anything like that again,' he said grimly, 'and you're the one who'll get beaten. I'll beat the daylights out of you!' He bundled his coat around her, and when she protested he said, 'I'm tinker-scum, I don't catch cold.'

They got back to the car, almost running, but even so Dora was starting to shiver. The car was warm and

Tip was sitting on her feet, but by the time they reached the village her teeth were chattering, and when Coll drove past the lodge she could hardly get out, 'You've p-passed it.'

'Shurrup!' he growled. He was in a foul temper, and she couldn't blame him. He was soaking wet too and he hadn't wanted to go swimming. She felt sobered up now, but she didn't feel repentant. She had enjoyed that. It had been a long time since she had done anything crazy and impetuous, and it was gratifying to have shaken Coll up so much that he was still fuming. For a change she had whistled and he had jumped. More or less. He had made her swim back, but she had made him jump into the river.

Inside the Manor, he ordered, 'Get yourself a hot bath.'

'Yes, sir.' She agreed that she needed a bath, to warm her up and wash away the river stickiness. She went into the first bathroom—there had been two in the old days, there was a third now, dating from the guesthouse. She soaped and soaked herself, then she washed her bra, pants and slip, hanging them on the heated towel rail, and came out swaddled in a huge white towel.

The house was warm and the bath had been hot, but she was still shivering, and she was afraid she was in for a chill. That midnight swim had been a daft thing to do, no matter how much she had enjoyed it. If she went down with the 'flu, or started sniffing and sneezing all over the place, Coll was going to be very tetchy tomorrow and she might wish she had been less headstrong tonight.

She didn't have a change of clothing here, but she had an overall and a mackintosh and a pair of wellies.

If she put them all on, and her long white dress and her shawl, she could walk home fast; though it might be more sense to take her old room for the night and get into bed as quickly as possible. If she could take a hot drink up with her, and find a couple of aspirins, she might ward off the worst of the threatened chill.

She went down into the kitchen where Coll was waiting for a kettle to boil. He was wearing a bathrobe, he had just had a bath too, and he turned a glowering face on her. She'd be safe enough sleeping here tonight. He didn't look in the least as though he wanted to seduce her.

She said meekly, 'I can't very well walk home like this. Can I have my old room?'

'You'd better, and you'd better have a hot drink.' Her teeth were chattering again and he said irascibly, 'Get yourself off, I'll bring it up to you.'

'Th-thank you.' She tried to point out that the blame was not all hers. 'There was no need for you to jump in. I wasn't drowning, I was waving.'

If she had hoped for a glimmer of a smile she didn't get it. He said, with a cutting edge to every word, 'I'm quite aware of that. And that you'd rather drown than reach for me.'

Dora pondered on that as she got into bed and pulled the bedclothes up to her chin. Her head wasn't quite as clear as she had thought it was, she *had* drunk too much, and when she closed her eyes a swirling, floating sensation, not entirely unpleasant, took over.

If she had been in difficulties in the river of course she would have reached for Coll. He must have thought she was, and it had been decent of him to dive in. Although he could hardly have let her get swept away over the weir, that would have taken some explaining.

She felt as though she was still floating, swimming. If only she could get really warm she would be asleep in no time. She was almost asleep now, and when Coll walked in she smiled sleepily at him.

He was terribly good-looking. She wished he liked her, because it was stupid not to like each other. He put a beaker on the table by her bed and went to turn on the electric fire. He said nothing and he moved quietly, and it was ridiculous to walk out without saying a word, which was what he was doing.

As he reached the door she said, 'Coll,' and when he turned, 'I wouldn't rather drown than reach for you.'

She held out a hand and he came back and took it in his hand. 'You're cold,' he said.

She said, 'Warm me,' and he sat down on the bed beside her and held her against him, gently stroking her back and shoulders. Dora snuggled closer, warmed and comforted by the feel and the smell of his smooth skin under the rough bathrobe, while a sweet sensuous languor was draining her of consciousness.

Her eyes were closed, her lids and limbs were heavy. She murmured, 'Hold me,' as though she was warm so long as his arms were around her, and then the velvet darkness covered her like a lover, and she slipped into a deep and dreamless sleep.

CHAPTER EIGHT

DORA woke, warm, curled up, cuddling a pillow against her cheek. Her eyes opened slowly, widening as her mind began ticking, until she was trying frantically to peer over her shoulder without moving her head. She couldn't, nor could she hear anything, and the bed felt empty, except for herself.

Very cautiously she raised her head and there was no dark head, no long shape under the bedclothes. She sat up, shivering, feeling less muzzy than last night but a long way from brilliant. Thick. Stupid. Having difficulty in marshalling her memories beyond what might well have been the point of no return.

Coll had been here. She remembered that very plainly, and she had been in his arms, but between then and now she didn't know. She didn't even know what time it was. Tommy and Mrs Heaton could be downstairs, and it would certainly start tongues wagging if she was found here without a stitch of clothing within reach.

She pulled back the curtains, blinking at the impact of daylight. It was broad daylight, which meant it could be anything from around eight o'clock. Coll could still be in the house, or he could have left. But she had to get dressed, and she badly needed a cup of coffee.

There were clothes on a chair, the undies she had washed and left to dry—they were dry now; and her shoes, pretty strappy evening sandals, and a button-up overall. If Coll had brought those in he had probably gone, and that was an ordeal postponed; she wasn't up

160

to facing him yet. By this evening she might be, although she was not convinced that there would ever be a time when she would be able to look him in the face again.

She crept into the bathroom. The only sound in the house was from Tip trotting along beside her. Dora looked wearily at him and said, 'It's a pity you can't talk, you might tell me how much of a fool I made of myself,' and then, 'Or it might be a jolly good job that you can't. Probably the less said about it the better.'

Downstairs in the kitchen was the coffee cup and the plate from which Coll had breakfasted, and the clock said half past eight, so Tommy was due any minute; he always arrived between half eight and nine, and Mrs Heaton and the gardener around nine o'clock.

Dora made herself a cup of instant coffee and then took it upstairs. She went to Coll's room, feeling a little as she did walking into the dentist's surgery, only much worse. She could hardly turn the door knob, in her other hand the cup was rattling in the saucer, and she stopped for another gulp of coffee in the corridor before she screwed up her courage enough to open the door.

She didn't need to go in. She could see the bed, smooth, unruffled, unslept in. She shut the door again and went to the room she had slept in for years, and it seemed last night with Coll, because she could be alone in there for a few minutes.

She couldn't face Tommy and Mrs Heaton, she couldn't face anyone until she had had time to pull herself together. She made herself drink the coffee. As she put the cup and saucer on the dressing table she saw the note, 'Thank you, you were fantastic,' and screwed it into a tight little ball and dropped it in the wastepaper basket.

She made the bed with nerveless hands, then sat down on it because her legs were boneless. So was her whole body. Her spine curved and she sat with her head in her hands, trying to remember.

She could remember that she had called Coll back from the door, and he had taken her hand and said it was cold. She remembered his touch and the comfort of his caress, stroking her hair and shoulders. For a moment she was lost in sensation, melting, then she jerked herself back and on to her feet, pacing up and down, scolding herself.

What a *stupid* thing to do, and she couldn't even remember. Although she concentrated until her head was throbbing she couldn't get past the image of Coll holding her and stroking her, and her feeling that she was safe, and home.

Safe! She nearly burst into hysterical laughter. There was no safety for her with him around. He was dangerous to her, her only enemy.

She was shivering, and she certainly couldn't go around all day dressed in a nylon overall and a pair of evening shoes. She'd better get home to the lodge and get dressed, so she went running down the stairs, just as she had when she had been dashing to the Fleece to accuse Coll of stealing her pearls. She didn't believe that any more, but she believed almost anything else about him. He was an unscrupulous opportunist, a taker. Probably the only reason he didn't take her pearls was because they weren't there to be stolen. She'd gone off wearing them.

She passed Tommy on his bicycle and he called,

'Morning, Miss Dora, what's the hurry?'

She was astonished that she should sound so cheerful and normal when she was feeling so confused and chaotic. When she got home she looked at herself in the mirror as though there should be some change, some sign in her face, but there wasn't. She put on her make-up, and a sweater and skirt, and changed her shoes; then she buttoned up the overall again and went back to the Manor.

She wouldn't think about last night because thinking wasn't making anything any clearer, and she'd keep very busy and get through the day that way.

In the library several shelves of old volumes had been replaced by Coll's books. Most of his books were even older, he had a collection of valuable first editions. The original books were worth hardly anything, but Dora had thought it might be an idea to catalogue them some time, and today seemed the day to do it.

The books that had been replaced were in a packing case in a store room and she made a list of titles and authors, then went into the library to start on the shelves.

It all gave an illusion of industry and concentration, although it was really a time-killer because she was scared of finding herself with breathing space.

She had lunch, as usual, with Mrs Heaton and Tommy, and Alex, a retired shepherd who came over three days a week to do the gardens, and after lunch Tommy asked her, 'Would you feel like giving Loki a run?'

Dora gave Loki his head across the heath, galloping full out, but for once she couldn't blow away her worries, and as the day ended and the time came when she would be seeing Coll again the stress continued to build up inside her until she hardly knew what she was doing.

What on earth *was* she going to do? Just suppose she and Coll had made love last night, could she carry it off as though she had had a string of lovers? What with riding and athletics it was unlikely she was still technically a virgin, only morally, but how could she act that kind of sophistication with any credibility? How could she pretend to be blasé and cynical when she wasn't, never had been and never would be? If only she *knew* what had happened!

She didn't want to be alone with him, but she couldn't bluff this out with Simon or Thea or anyone else listening. It was Friday evening and they usually came round on Friday evenings, but she had phoned them as soon as she got back from her ride over the heath and said that Coll was bringing work home tonight, how about them coming tomorrow?

'Yes, sure,' said Thea. 'Everything all right?'

'Much as usual,' said Dora, and bit her lip hard.

The meal was ready and she was still in the library when Coll arrived. Tip went to meet him and brought him to where she was, standing at a table jotting down titles and authors in alphabetical order. Dora said brightly, 'I've started cataloguing the books.'

She finished the line she was writing and straightened up; and he looked at her with that slow up-and-down look, and what was behind it this time? Triumph? Amusement?

'Hello,' he said.

'Hello.' She put down her ball-point pen, waiting for a couple of seconds to make sure it wasn't going to roll off the table, feeling as though she was doing everything in slow motion. Very deliberately she pushed the papers tidily together and said, 'Dinner's ready,' and then, slowly, she turned towards him.

She had to walk past him to leave the room, and she knew he was going to block her way. He put an arm across the door, leaning against the side so that she would have to duck under his arm to get out.

'Dinner's always ready,' he said. 'You're a marvellous cook, an extraordinary woman.' The dark eyes gleamed under the dark lashes. 'But until last night I didn't quite realise how extraordinary.'

Dora drew in a quick breath. 'All that experience certainly pays off,' he added softly. 'Such versatility!'

'Which is more than I can say for your experience,' she said tartly. 'I can't remember a thing.'

'You can't?' His expression of horror was too stricken to be true. 'None of it? Shall I refresh your memory? I'm sure something will come back to you if we run over the ground again.'

She hoped he was teasing her, she wished she had the strength to be flippant and pretend she didn't care. But she did care, and she asked huskily, 'Please, what did happen?'

He dropped the arm that was barring her way out and shrugged, 'Nothing, I'm sorry to say. You were sleeping like a baby, so I tucked you up and left you.'

She was profoundly relieved for about four seconds, then she remembered, 'You didn't sleep in your own bed.'

Coll grinned. 'I made it this morning. I thought that and the thank-you note might give you something to think about. I owed you something for last night's dip.'

She had had a day she wouldn't forget in a hurry.

She was furious with him, and deep down a little aggrieved as though it was no compliment that he had tucked her up and left her. Anyhow, she could do her blasé act now with an easy mind.

'Well,' she drawled, 'you couldn't have wanted to seduce me very badly.'

'I do like a little co-operation,' he drawled too, one dark eyebrow raised, long mouth quirked at the corner. 'You were out to the world.'

She was. If she had slept less heavily she would have known she had slept peacefully and alone. 'All that wine you made me drink,' she muttered resentfully, and he fell back a pace.

'*I* made you drink? A fine lot of influence I had on you last night, swimming in the weir stretch at midnight. That was what laid you out.'

'Nonsense!' Although he could well be right. She said firmly, 'That did me no harm at all, it was lovely. Nothing better for the health than swimming,' and suddenly she sneezed.

She had been sniffing and sneezing all day, but this sneeze caught her by surprise and Coll began to laugh, and after she had dabbed her nose with a tissue Dora admitted, 'Somehow I do seem to have caught a cold. I suppose I can't blame that on the wine.'

They ate the evening meal together, and watched a play on television, then Dora said it was time she took herself and her sniffles home.

'You won't stay here?' Coll asked, and she laughed, but blushed as well, remembering what an idiot she had been.

'Thanks, but no, I won't push my luck.'

'You were lucky, Dora-Lily, you picked the right time to flake out.' He was smoking a cigar, the pale blue smoke rising and the erotic male smell of it in the air. Dora was getting used to the drawing room the way it was now, to Coll being master of the house. It would have been nice to stay instead of turning out and walking down the drive to the lodge, which was cold these days because she was rarely in there long enough to bother lighting fires.

She had been eating shortbread biscuits, it had been a cosy evening. She said, 'Come on, Tip.'

These days Tip seemed to consider himself as much Coll's dog as Dora's, and Coll encouraged him. He was Coll's pet, and perhaps Dora was becoming his pet too. Perhaps she entertained and amused him as the little dog did.

Maybe he wanted her, but not all that desperately, or last night when she was lying in his arms he would have kissed her and woken her and made love to her. Not desperately at all, and she got up and brushed a few crumbs off her skirt. 'Come on,' she said again to the little dog who didn't want to leave the fire, nor Coll, it seemed. 'Time to go home.'

When they were children Christmas had been a special time of year at the Manor House. There had been a magnificent tree in the hall, reaching higher than the gallery. There had been a splendid party, and guests staying on for New Year's Eve. Plans for Christmas had started as soon as they were into the month of November, but not this year, and this year November was cold and miserable.

Everyone seemed slightly depressed at the onset of winter, and Dora was no exception. She was busy enough, but it was depressing weather, a lot of drizzle which took the pleasure out of riding and darkened the house so that you had to keep lights on all day long. As Christmas came nearer she wondered whether there would be any celebrations in the house, if she should ask Coll what his plans were.

As it turned out she didn't have to ask. She was outside with Coll, talking to Tommy about some repairs needed on the stable roof, and it was cold, their breath was frosting in the air.

'Nippy this morning,' said Tommy. 'Christmas'll be on us before we know it.' They both agreed with him and he sighed and grinned nostalgically. 'Ah, we had some grand Christmasses here in the old days, didn't we, Miss Dora?'

Dora's eyes lit with memories. 'Didn't we just?'

Even that last Christmas there had been the tree and the trimmings and the guests. Laurence Holcroft had lived in style to the end.

'It's a family house, is this,' Tommy had gone on, 'needs children around. It's too big for a bachelor.' He had given Coll a sly grin and Coll had grinned back at him,

'You think so?'

Dora had dug her hands deep into her pockets. Tommy was hinting it was time that Coll married her. Tommy expected her and Coll to provide the family to fill the old house with laughter again, and there wasn't a chance, not a hope. Amusement and edgy antagonism were all they were ever likely to share.

Coll would probably marry some time and his children would live here, tall and dark and beautiful and clever; and she would marry herself, she supposed. She supposed. She walked away from them and left them talking about the roof.

Coll caught her a few minutes later in the kitchen

and said, 'About Christmas. Tommy says you always had a Christmas party.'

Coll had always come in the summer, he had never been here for Christmas, but he was here now and she was waiting for his orders. She said, 'We did.'

'Let's do that,' he said. 'Could you manage it?'

'Of course.'

'Right, I'll make a list of my guests and you and Thea and Simon ask who you want.'

'Thank you,' she said. She didn't think Coll heard her. He was looking preoccupied; not worried, but as though he was planning, making decisions.

Simon and Thea were delighted, Simon in particular. 'You've never seen the old house at its best,' he told Thea. 'We had terrific Christmasses, didn't we?'

'Always,' said Dora.

'A great big tree,' Simon went on. 'How about that, then?' to Kiki. 'Instead of that two-foot phoney in the box in the broom cupboard.'

They usually had a family Christmas in the flat. It was always festive and fun, but this was going to be Christmas on the old scale and it was grand to phone up friends and invite them to the Manor for a Christmas Day party.

Everyone accepted, there wasn't a refusal. 'How about Neil?' Simon suggested, fooling, and when Dora said,

'Don't you dare, I'm going to have enough to do organising everything, I don't need any diversions,' he said, pretending to be impressed,

'But of course, you're the hostess.'

It looked like that. The local guests were her friends, but in fact she was not the hostess. She was the housekeeper, paid for what she was doing. She had to consult Coll and get his consent at every stage, and he seemed determined that everything should go smoothly and that the house should look as spectacular as possible.

When guests had come down previously, usually for weekends, he had left everything to Dora, but this time he was carrying on as though it must all be perfect. As if this time he wanted to make an impression, and she wondered—on whom?

But he gave her no clue until she handed over the guest lists. He hardly glanced at the names of her guests. 'Fine,' he said. But his guests—and there were a dozen of them—would all be staying for a couple of nights, several for longer, so Dora had had to give a lot of attention to their names.

She had met them all but one, and that name headed Coll's list. Loretta Corbishley. She sat and looked at that for a while, and then she got on with the task of allotting bedrooms. She put Loretta, who wasn't paired off with anyone else, into the little room that used to be her own, and showed Coll the list that night.

As he began to make changes she leaned over to see what they were. He was putting Loretta in the room next to his and Dora stood back, with folded arms, while he juggled with the rest. He had to alter a few, but where Loretta was sleeping was his main concern, and when he handed back the list Dora said casually, 'She hasn't been down here before, has she?'

'No.' She waited and he said, 'We always spend Christmas together. Christmas is a special time for us.'

She wanted to ask, 'Why?' but there was a note in his voice that was like tenderness, and there was a pain in her that was like jealousy, so that she couldn't trust herself to say anything.

She felt she knew then who all the fuss was for. This house would be like a fairy palace on Christmas Day, and if Loretta Corbishley wasn't enchanted she was hard to please.

They were getting in temporary staff over the holiday, which meant that Dora could sit down with the resident guests for Christmas lunch, there was a super buffet laid on for the party. When she asked Coll where he wanted everyone seated he suggested she or Thea took the seat at the bottom of the table, traditionally that of hostess, but the only place on which he had firm instructions was that Loretta Corbishley should sit next to him.

Dora made no comment at all. She made a note, and then she made out the place names, and not even Thea knew that Coll had given any special orders about Miss Corbishley.

The preparations went on and Christmas was nearly here, with nobody talking about anything else. Mrs Heaton came downstairs the week before Christmas, smiling broadly, and took Dora on one side to whisper that she had seen Coll's present for Dora.

She looked so impressed that it had to be something expensive, and Dora wished it wasn't. They owed him enough. She didn't want a pricey present, even if it was in the nature of a farewell gift because at the end of next month she would have reached her six-month target.

She was rushing about a great deal, involving herself in every little detail of the future festivities, but she was feeling as flat as pond water. All the excitement was going over her head, and she longed for the whole thing to be over.

It would take more than a present, no matter how splendid, to thrill her right now. She was tired, she supposed. Once she had got her six months over and done with she might take a holiday, and then another job away from here. She was feeling so depressed that she wondered if she might be heading for some sort of illness, she felt so sick of it all.

But her present, when she got it, jolted her out of her inertia of spirit.

A couple of nights before Christmas Eve Simon and Thea arrived with Coll's present. There would be a lot of gift exchanging later, and they felt that theirs would stand a better chance of appreciation if they handed it over early. They were proud of having found it, because it was a first edition of Dickens' *Bleak House* and Coll was delighted with it.

Then he brought down their gifts. They were in the drawing room and Simon unwrapped a cashmere sweater, and Thea a beautifully embroidered shawl. There was a large box of gifts for Kiki's stocking, and Dora's was in a flat oblong leather box.

She lifted the lid on a string of pearls and sat looking at them while Simon tried on his sweater and Thea paraded in her shawl. It was a finer string than her mother's pearls, but she knew they were what Coll was replacing, and she felt the blood draining out of her face as though she was looking at a ghost.

They all seemed to be ghosts, she and Simon and Coll, and she was walking to a mirror, as she had done all those years ago, fumbling to fasten the pearls around her neck.

She heard Thea gasp, 'Oh, Dora, they're beautiful!'

Dora's fingers trembled, she hadn't even thought to look how the fastener worked, and then Coll came up behind her and she felt his fingers against the nape of her neck, his breath on her cheek.

This had happened before. The last time he had tried to fasten the pearls for her, when she was sixteen, and her heart had beat so loud she had thought he must hear it.

He said, 'To replace the ones you never found.'

She couldn't turn to look at him. She could only look at him in the mirror, the proud hawk face; and inside her was a wild confusion as though she was sixteen again, afraid of her feelings, unsure what was happening to her, wishing that Simon would go away.

Then she saw Simon's reflection. His face was scarlet, a picture of guilt and misery, and Thea walked in front of him, pretending to peer into the mirror too. 'I want to see how I look full length,' Thea said. There were long mirrors in the wardrobes in the bedrooms. She slipped her hand through Dora's arm and coaxed, 'Come and look at yourself full length in your pearls.'

Dora went with her. She would have gone with anyone who took her hand, she was so shocked that for a moment she had no will of her own, but as they went into the first bedroom and Thea opened the wardrobe door Dora asked, 'How long have you known?'

'That Simon took the pearls? Ever since you told me you'd lost them.'

Neither girl was looking at her reflection. They were looking at each other, and without speaking Dora was asking—why?

'He was a spender,' said Thea. 'He was a gambler when I first met him.' He didn't gamble now, but while he was at college it could have been different.

'Then suddenly he had enough to pay off a bookmaker who was pressing him,' said Thea. 'Just about the time you lost your pearls.'

She pulled the shawl tighter around her, her eyes pleading for understanding. 'When your father died in such terrible debt it was the shock that Simon needed. It made him pull himself together. It steadied him.'

Thea's influence had probably done as much as anything. Dora had had no idea that Simon had needed money so badly—he hadn't confided in her as he had in Thea. She said, 'I'd have given them to him. He shouldn't have taken them. Not then. Not so that it looked as though it might have been Coll.'

He had timed it. He had thought that Coll was clearing off and they wouldn't be seeing him again for years. He shouldn't have done that, although he had tried to make Dora believe she had worn them and lost them.

'No,' said Thea, in a very small voice.

'Do you think Coll guessed?' Dora asked.

'I guess so,' said Thea, and Dora laughed because she could have wept.

'Coll can't have a very high opinion of either Simon or me, but I think he likes you.'

'He likes us all,' said Thea.

'Maybe.' Dora was far from convinced of that. 'If I was him I wouldn't,' she said, and Thea begged,

'Please don't say anything.'

What would be the use now? No wonder Simon had never mentioned Coll in all these years, his conscience must still worry him. He must have been thankful that the subject of the pearls—so far as he knew—had never come up again. He must have thought that Coll had gone away without hearing anything about them, and that Dora had forgotten them, or at any rate wasn't blaming anyone else for their loss.

She put an arm around Thea and hugged her. 'I always knew you were the saving of Simon. It's lucky for him you're a one-man woman.'

'And for me,' said Thea softly. 'It's better that way.'

'I'm sure it is,' said Dora. If the man loved you ...

Dora didn't get much sleep that night. The pearls, and the moment when Coll put them around her neck, had unlocked the past. Now she really could remember how she had felt at sixteen.

There had always been an awareness between herself and Coll that had expressed itself in conflict. But the last time he came, when she was sixteen, she had been ready to fall in love with him.

She had had crushes on boy-friends, slight cheerful things, but when Coll came that time she had been tongue-tied with a strange shyness. When he had touched her, trying to fasten her pearls, it had felt as though a hundred electric shocks were coursing through her. All she had wanted to do was turn to him and throw her arms around him.

She had been an unsophisticated sixteen-year-old. She had got out of the room as fast as she could, and gone riding instead of going to the party. She had felt wild and free and strong and beautiful, while she was galloping over the heath, and her blood was singing. But when she came back she couldn't go into the room where Coll and Simon were talking together and music was playing.

She had crept up to her own room, and stayed there as night came down. Perhaps Coll was staying the night, perhaps when everyone else was asleep he would tap on her door or throw gravel up to her window, and she would open the door or the window, and then he would tell her he had come to see her, not Simon. Perhaps he would kiss her and say he had thought about her often.

But of course he didn't come, and she had tossed restless and fearful. She had wanted Coll and she had been afraid of wanting him, because it would be terrible if he laughed at her, she would die of shame.

She was both child and woman that night, unprepared for the longings that were assailing her; but when morning came, cool and grey, she had reminded herself how little she knew of him. It was years since they had seen him, and this time he had hardly spoken to her, or looked at her except when he tried to fasten her pearls.

He had looked at her pearls as though they were beautiful, but not at her, and she had gone downstairs for a glass of milk and her pearls weren't where she had left them.

She had remembered again how Coll had looked at them, and when Simon had said he had gone, and he wasn't coming back, she had been sick at the thought that he might have taken them. She had run all the way to the Fleece, and he had stared at her with eyes as narrow as the eyes in a mask, and when she had said, 'You wouldn't have picked up my pearls last night, would you?' he had grinned and said, 'Prove it.'

She had despised herself then, remembering her dreams of the night before. She had wanted to hit out at him, to scream at him. She had thought she hated him and would always hate him. But ever since, some part of her, deep down, had been measuring every man she met against him. That was why she couldn't give herself completely, because they weren't Coll. She had been waiting for Coll, and she might have gone on waiting for the rest of her life.

She might have decided she was frigid, a loner. Well, she knew now that she was neither, but knowing herself was going to make life no easier when Loretta Corbishley came at Christmas, sitting by Coll at the table, sleeping in the room next to his.

The days were going to be grim enough, but the nights—when Dora was lying alone in her cold little house, seeing them in her mind, seeing everything through the long sleepless hours—would be infinitely worse.

Next day the Christmas rush went on. The tree was in the hall now and it would take most of the morning to dress it. There were boxes of trimmings, and with the aid of a high stepladder Dora was transforming its dark green branches into a bright and glittering spectacle.

She was unravelling tinsel when Mrs Heaton came into the hall. 'It's going to be pretty,' said Mrs Heaton, admiring the tree. 'This is going to be a red-letter Christmas, isn't it?' She smiled as though she and Dora shared a secret, and dropped her voice although nobody else was about. 'When you get your present from the master.'

'I had it last night,' said Dora, and Mrs Heaton's secret smile widened.

'You did? Oh ... but you're not wearing it.' She sounded disappointed, looking at Dora's left hand, then she whispered again, 'Saving it for Christmas Day? I won't tell anyone. I'm not supposed to know, but when I saw the little box on his dressing table I couldn't resist taking a little peep.' She sighed ecstatically. 'My, but it is a *beautiful* ring!'

She went on her way, upstairs, and Dora stood, stunned. Then she dropped the tinsel back in the box and went into the library, closing the door and sitting at the desk that was covered with lists and notes and Christmas wrapping paper.

A ring! A beautiful ring! For Loretta, of course. On Christmas Day, when the house was at its beautiful best and the party was laid on, Loretta would be beside Coll, wearing his ring.

He should have told her. He should have warned her. Everyone she and Simon had invited thought that Dora and Coll were lovers, that the Manor was Dora's home again. If Coll had wanted to hurt her pride this should do it. No matter how she protested that she didn't care they would always believe that she had been jilted in her turn, and the ones who remembered Peter, and the wedding she had called off at the last minute, might say she knew now how it felt.

And she did, she did. She hoped with all her heart that Peter hadn't cared for her as she cared for Coll, because it was like no other pain on earth. It didn't matter who laughed at her or pitied her, that wasn't why she felt as though she—was sitting here slowly dying.

It was because she knew now that she would never belong to Coll, nor he to her. He was going away again, as far as he could go although he would still be living in this house.

She wondered, for about the hundredth time, what Loretta Corbishley was like. Coll had mentioned a girl who looked something like Dora. Perhaps she would see someone who looked like herself living here with

Coll, sharing the children. Coll's children and some-one else's.

She felt as though her own children had been torn away from her, as though all her future had been laid barren because her future should have been Coll. Whether he wanted her or not, and he didn't, she was inextricably bound to him, and he must never know that. Nobody must ever know.

Christmas was a special time for him and Loretta. 'We always spend Christmas together,' he had said. Perhaps they had first met at Christmas, and this Christmas he was asking her to marry him.

That was why everything had to be perfect, why he had seemed on edge lately. Perhaps he wasn't certain she would accept him, but she would. Dora was as sure of that as she was sure that she herself wouldn't be around to see it.

Everything was organised down to the last detail, so that Dora could be free over the holiday to enjoy her-self like the other guests. *Enjoy* herself? It would be murder. She would be dying the death of a thousand cuts. Oh no! Oh no, no, *no*.

They would all guess why she wasn't around, but she would handle that when she came back. When the engagement was a few days old and less of a thrilling, exciting surprise she would face them all and smile, and not cry in front of anyone, except Thea perhaps. But today she couldn't even tell Thea.

She took out the A.A. book and phoned what seemed to be dozens of small hotels around the coun-try before she got a cancelled booking for the Christ-mas break. Then she got down to tying up the loose ends of the celebrations at the Manor House.

She finished the tree and she finished wrapping the

parcels; there was a gift for every guest at the party. She put the final touches to the decorations of gold and silver, with an occasional splash of scarlet, so that the whole house was glittering and shining and ready for tomorrow, when the guests would start arriving and she would leave very very early for her small hotel on the south coast.

She had to tell Simon and Thea, of course. They had been busy with Christmas shoppers all day, but she would go along tonight after she had seen Coll. She hoped he would come home early, but he didn't.

It was quite late when Tip gave warning of his car, and she was alone. The lights in the hall were reflected in baubles and tinsel and she was in the hall, piling up the presents at the foot of the tree.

She felt quite calm, numb, as though she had taken a handful of tranquillisers. She had heard of that happening to people who were badly injured and she hoped it would last until she was back in her own home.

Coll came into the hall, and stood quite near her, looking around, smiling. 'It is rather splendid, isn't it?' he said.

'Yes, it is.' Dora balanced another parcel. 'Can I talk to you?'

'What about?' He walked towards the drawing room. 'Wait while I get a drink. The traffic's solid on the motorway tonight.' As he didn't come back she followed him, he was standing by the fireplace. Of course it was cold outside, although there were no signs yet of this being a white Christmas, more an iron grey one. 'Now,' he said, 'what's the matter?'

He thought something had gone wrong with the preparations, that things would be less than perfect for

Loretta, and Dora said sharply, 'Don't worry, everything's organised, everything will go like clockwork. It's just that I won't be here.'

'*What?*' He glared at her. The skin on his face looked taut and white across the cheekbones and round the mouth, and she muttered,

'I'm spending Christmas somewhere else, that's all.'

Coll swore through lips that hardly moved, as though he was in two minds about hurling the tumbler he held against the wall. Or perhaps at her because he had been robbed of a little triumph, he had wanted her around to meet Loretta. Dora wondered if he knew how cruel he was.

Instead he put down the tumbler on the mantelpiece and said harshly, 'All right, now, what exactly are you saying?'

She gripped her hands together and got out the words. 'I want to finish. I want to stop working for you. I don't want to come back.'

'Why?'

'Because I'm not the stuff of which martyrs are made.' She had taken enough, she wasn't waiting for the *coup de grâce*. She asked, 'Can I go?' and he said savagely,

'You can go to hell!'

'Thank you,' she said. 'Yes.' That was funny. That was where she was. 'You're sacking me, are you?' she said.

'What?'

'I owe you another month.' She didn't believe he would punish Simon and Thea, but she asked, 'What about the money they owe you if I go?'

He winced, as though struck by a spasm of physical pain, over in a flash but leaving him bone white under the tan, and she almost ran towards him. 'Coll, what is it? Are you ill?'

He backed from her outstretched hand before she could reach him. 'Would you mind not touching me?' That stopped her. 'What do you think I'm made of?' and as she gasped he almost shouted at her, 'You can't go. You've got to be here at Christmas. What do you think all this is for?'

'Loretta?' she gulped.

'What about Loretta?'

'You're getting engaged to her, aren't you?'

'I shouldn't think she'd have me.'

'Why not?' Had she turned him down? Might she turn him down?

'For one thing, there's an age gap of forty years,' he said drily. 'She's seventy.'

Dora wanted to laugh—she was laughing. She staggered to the sofa and sat down limply, and Coll came and sat beside her. 'Who is she?' she asked.

'Loretta? When I was on the building site one of the blokes I worked with was Bill Corbishley. She was his great-aunt, she'd reared him and they were good to me. I spent a lot of time at their house, I always went there for Christmas.

'Bill was killed the year I started up in business on my own, and I still spend Christmas with Loretta. Or she spends it with me. This is a big house, there'll be a lot of folk around, she'll be happier in a room next to mine.'

Dora was feeling reborn. All the hope and confidence that had drained out of her in the last few weeks was coming back. She couldn't wait to meet Loretta. She asked, 'Where does she live?'

'In Walsall, where she's always lived. In a bungalow I built for her.'

That was nice. Miss Corbishley would be nice too. Dora was staying here for Christmas now, she was staying as long as there was a flicker of hope.

Coll was still pale, she could feel the tension in him as he watched her, and her own nerves tightened as she asked, 'What are you giving her for Christmas?'

'We're still talking about Loretta?' He grinned slightly. 'A new carpet for her bedroom, covered with pink roses. Why?'

Dora ran her tongue along her dry lips. 'Who's the ring for?' He frowned and she whispered, 'Mrs Heaton saw it on your dressing table.' She had to know, but perhaps she shouldn't have asked. Her mouth was so dry that she couldn't swallow and the lump in her throat was stopping her breath.

Coll sat a little way from her, long legs jack-knifed, hands clasped loosely together across bony knees. He wasn't looking at her any more, he was looking down. He said wryly, 'She nipped in pretty fast, it couldn't have been there more than ten minutes,' and then in sudden fierce impatience, 'Damn the woman, I didn't plan it like this.'

Dora tried to ask, 'Plan what?'

Coll was never at a loss for words, he always knew what he wanted to say, but he was floundering now, words and gestures jerky and erratic, hands clenching and unclenching.

'I thought—Christmas—that's the time, when the house is like it used to be. Christmas Eve—before they started to arrive I was going to say, 'You want the old place again, don't you? You can have it if you'll take me with it.'

Dora still couldn't breathe. She could only look and listen, as though any movement on her part and the moment would shatter like one of the fragile silver baubles on the Christmas tree.

Coll looked up then, and threw back his head in that do-or-die gesture, but this time there was no triumph in his eyes. He was afraid, terribly afraid. 'Will you marry me?' he said, and his lips were white.

'Do you love me?' She couldn't believe it, except that he looked like she had felt, as though someone else held his life in their hands.

'Too much,' he said. 'It's always been too much,' and she cried out,

'Don't say that!'

'You tear my heart out,' he muttered.

'You don't do mine much good,' she said shakily.

'Do you want the house?' They were face to face. His eyes were agonised and she leaned towards him.

'Of course,' she said. 'I like it—I love it. But any other house would do. I want you. I don't much care where I live, but I've been waiting for you for ten whole years.'

His arms came around her and she met his lips fiercely. They kissed with a starving hunger, and then she lay, eyes closed, in the crook of his arm, while he kissed her very softly and gently, brow and eyelids, cheeks and throat.

Everywhere he touched her her body quickened, and the dark head bowed and his lips burned against her breast. She had suspended all control, she would have responded naturally and joyfully to her clamorous senses, she wanted their lovemaking completed, and when Coll raised his head she almost drew him close again. But then she smiled, because they had a lifetime of loving ahead.

'Do you know what brought me back here?' he asked.

'The advertisement for the house.'

'The announcement of your engagement.' As she blinked he explained, 'I saw it in the *Telegraph*.'

... Mrs Hewitt might not have been enthusiastic about her darling boy getting married, but she was a great one for the social niceties. She had sent in that announcement, and paid for it, and Dora wondered if she would ever have the nerve to thank her for it ...

'And I realised that the girl I was going around with looked like you,' said Coll. 'All of them had.' He ran a tingling fingertip around the oval of her face. 'There aren't many girls who look like you,' he said, 'but those were the ones I found.'

Her chin cupped comfortably in his hand. 'Only none of them were you,' he said, 'and that was what was wrong with them. So I came back here.'

'Me too,' she said softly. 'That was what was wrong with my lot. So you came back. Thank heaven you came back!'

'Amen,' he said, not smiling, but as though he really was thanking heaven. He said, 'There was a For Sale board up at the house, so I thought I'd look round and ask about you, and when I saw you again I knew there was no easy way. I wasn't going to say hello and good-bye and walk away cured. But I thought that if I kept you around for six months I might get you out of my system.'

'But you haven't?' she asked for the joy of hearing him say,

'I never will. You're too deep inside me. For the first week it was enough to needle you and see your eyes flash. I'd rather fight with you than make love with any other woman, but long before you dived into the weir I knew that I'd die for you.'

She would die for him. She didn't want to race against him, she wanted to go with him wherever he went, anywhere, everywhere. She wanted to tell him about ten years ago, and she put her lips to his cheek and asked him,

'Why didn't you tell me you hadn't seen the pearls? I was falling in love with you, only I didn't know how to handle it, I wasn't prepared. I was in a dreadful mix-up, but if you'd put your arms around me I'd have followed you, back to the building site or wherever you were going.'

'Would you?' When he looked at her like that she felt an explosion of happiness that she could hardly contain. 'I'd come back to ask you to wait for me,' he said, 'but I couldn't. I could hardly look at you, I couldn't get a word out. I sat up all night writing you a letter, promising I was going to make a fortune for you, because it had always been you ever since I fell out of that tree.

'I had it stamped and addressed, ready to drop into the local letter box, then I was going back to my digs to sweat it out. Only you came charging in to tell me I'd pinched your pearls, so I tore it up and thanked God I hadn't posted it, and swore I'd never write another love letter so long as I lived.'

'Thea guessed it was Simon. She said he owed money to a bookmaker.' Dora felt her brother's guilt as though some measure of it was her own, and she tried to smile. 'I only realised last night and I promised her

I wouldn't do anything about it, but do you think she'd mind if I changed my mind and killed him?'

Coll laughed. 'I'd mind. I like old Simon.'

'I'm glad about that.' She was glad of many things, most of all of the tender and passionate love that had always been waiting for her in Coll. She was so glad about that that she could have swooned from joy.

'Dora-Lily,' he said, and put a strand of her hair to his lips. It didn't annoy her now, it sounded like a caress. He said, 'I wanted a name for you that no one else used. All those years ago I wanted us to be sharing, even when we were scrapping.'

Her eyes were bright, with love and with laughter. 'The fighting was fun, wasn't it?'

'I enjoyed it.' He laughed in her hair. His breath tickled her ear and she said,

'As much as making love?'

'I didn't say that. I said I'd rather fight you than love any other woman.' His face was very close to her face. She looked deep into his eyes and saw absolute love, and even the years of waiting seemed wonderful because they had been leading to this. 'But I'd rather make love with you,' he said, 'than rule the world.'

Dora had no past experience to draw on, but with Coll she would know all she needed to know, everything, because she felt that way too, that he was her kingdom and her home.

'Yes,' she said, 'oh *yes*!' and she smiled as he kissed her.

 # Harlequin

COLLECTION
EDITIONS OF 1978

**50 great stories
of special beauty
and significance**

$1.25
each novel

In 1976 we introduced the first 100 Harlequin Collections—a selection of titles chosen from our best sellers of the past 20 years. This series, a trip down memory lane, proved how great romantic fiction can be timeless and appealing from generation to generation. The theme of love and romance is eternal, and, when placed in the hands of talented, creative, authors whose true gift lies in their ability to write from the heart, the stories reach a special level of brilliance that the passage of time cannot dim. Like a treasured heirloom, an antique of superb craftsmanship, a beautiful gift from someone loved—these stories too, have a special significance that transcends the ordinary. **$1.25 each novel**

Here are your 1978
Harlequin Collection Editions...

Original Harlequin Romance numbers in brackets

ORDER FORM
Harlequin Reader Service

In U.S.A.
MPO Box 707
Niagara Falls, N.Y. 14302

In Canada
649 Ontario St.,
Stratford, Ontario, N5A 6W2

Please send me the following Harlequin Collection
novels. I am enclosing my check or money order
for $1.25 for each novel ordered, plus 25¢ to cover
postage and handling.

☐ 102	☐ 115	☐ 128	☐ 140
☐ 103	☐ 116	☐ 129	☐ 141
☐ 104	☐ 117	☐ 130	☐ 142
☐ 105	☐ 118	☐ 131	☐ 143
☐ 106	☐ 119	☐ 132	☐ 144
☐ 107	☐ 120	☐ 133	☐ 145
☐ 108	☐ 121	☐ 134	☐ 146
☐ 109	☐ 122	☐ 135	☐ 147
☐ 110	☐ 123	☐ 136	☐ 148
☐ 111	☐ 124	☐ 137	☐ 149
☐ 112	☐ 125	☐ 138	☐ 150
☐ 113	☐ 126	☐ 139	☐ 151
☐ 114	☐ 127		

Number of novels checked @
$1.25 each = $ _____

N.Y. and N.J. residents add
appropriate sales tax $ _____

Postage and handling $ ____.25

TOTAL $ _____

NAME _____
(Please Print)

ADDRESS _____

CITY _____

STATE/PROV. _____

ZIP/POSTAL CODE _____

ROM 2187

Offer expires December 31, 1978